Gabrielle Kraft

PUBLISHED BY POCKET BOOKS NEW YORK

This novel is a work of fiction. Names, characters, places and incidents are either the product of the author's imagination or are used fictitiously. Any resemblance to actual events or locales or persons, living or dead, is entirely coincidental.

Another *Original* publication of POCKET BOOKS

POCKET BOOKS, a division of Simon & Schuster, In
1230 Avenue of the Americas, New York, N.Y. 10020

Copyright © 1987 by Gabrielle Kraft
Cover artwork copyright © 1987 Wil Cormier

ISBN: 0-671-63724-X

First Pocket Books printing October 1987

10 9 8 7 6 5 4 3 2 1

POCKET and colophon are registered trademarks
of Simon & Schuster, Inc.

Printed in the U.S.A.

. . . SOMEWHERE FAR, FAR AWAY, BEHIND WINK-en, Blinken, and Nod drifting peacefully in their pea-green boat, behind the Three Bears holed up in their cozy winter cave, a bell pealed in the sleepy village of Jerry Zalman's dreams . . .

"Oh my God!" the girl next to Zalman moaned. She was tall and blond and leggy and her name was Tammy something that Zalman couldn't recall as he reached out blindly for the phone. Finally he managed to knock the instrument off the antique marble-topped nightstand onto the Oriental carpet, where it stopped ringing.

"Zally? Zally? Are you there?" the phone asked.

Zalman sighed, took off his blue velvet sleep mask, and picked up the phone. "I hope this is good," he said. "I really do."

"Zally," Phil Hanning said cheerily. "I only called so maybe we'd run up to Finest Snax for breakfast, huh?"

Zalman sighed again and looked around his bedroom. On the opposite wall a framed poster of Jimmy Cagney as the Public Enemy snarled at Paul Muni as Scarface. Zalman loved his bedroom. In fact, he loved his entire house in the

5

Hollywood Hills. When he'd moved in after his last divorce he'd realized a fond dream: he finally had enough room for his extensive collection of gangster movie posters, key cards, and still photographs.

"What time is it, Phil?" Zalman asked. "No, don't tell me. Let me guess. It must be pretty early because I can see the sun through my east window." Through a part in the white satin draperies over sliding glass doors that looked out on the tile patio Zalman saw sunlight glinting off his swimming pool. He looked at the Dunhill clock he'd recently bought on sale for $248. It read eight o'clock. The girl moaned. "It's nothing, dear," Zalman said paternally. "It's only my crazy brother-in-law."

"Huh, Zally?" Hanning said. "Whaddya say?"

"Drop dead, Phil," Zalman said. He hung up the phone and replaced the sleep mask over his eyes. The girl shifted in her sleep and he felt the long, smooth expanse of her naked thigh as she cuddled up to him. Maybe the peaceful village of his dreams wasn't beyond reach. The phone rang again.

This time Zalman did not bother to remove the sleep mask. "What is it now, Phil?" he said unpleasantly.

"Jesus, Zally," Hanning moaned. "Don't hang up on me. You gotta help me. Lucille is gonna slaughter me if she finds out. And anyway it's all your fault."

Zalman lay silent and brooding behind his sleep mask. "Phil," he said patiently, "if my sister slaughters you the world will be minus a schmuck. So why should I get up out of a warm bed and go eat crummy deli food in order to save your life?"

"Quit kidding, will you, Zally," Hanning begged. "This is for real. I'm in a hell of a mess."

Zalman knew it was too late. Thanks to Phil Hanning he was awake. He took off the sleep mask and looked around to see Tammy gazing at him. Her wide blue orbs were aglow with the beauty of the night of passion he hoped they'd shared but which he somehow couldn't quite recall.

"I gotta pee," she giggled, struggling out of the huge bed. Despite the allure of her naked body, now disappearing into his bathroom, Zalman felt a familiar sinking sensation in his stomach. Was it the girls he went out with or was it a flaw in his own character?

"What the hell," Zalman sighed into the phone. "Okay, Phil, why not?"

An hour and a half later, showered, shaved, and wearing a tweed jacket over chinos and a blue work shirt, Zalman shot his perfectly restored 1968 silver-gray Mercedes 280 SE into a loading zone on Ventura Boulevard and headed for the Finest Snax, a barnlike eatery which advertised itself as the biggest and best delicatessen in the San Fernando Valley. He noticed a few people gathered around his sister's stainless steel DeLorean parked across the street, which meant that Hanning had already arrived. It was a point in his favor, Zalman thought grimly as he hustled down the gum-stained sidewalk past a row of vending machines dispensing pornographic newspapers.

Zalman was an attorney in Beverly Hills and knew he was touchy about some things, like waiting for people who were late. But he also knew that at thirty-five he was rich enough to afford his quirks. He was a good-looking guy with black curly hair, quizzical brown eyes, and a mocking grin and he had just about everything money could buy, except height. He was five foot five. Actually, he was only five foot four and a half, but he lied about the half inch. Naturally he was a little touchy on the subject, especially when girls told him he was cute, sort of like a sharp-featured version of Billy Joel.

The Finest Snax was jumping. It was filled with tennis players in shining whites, Sunday morning bagel buyers, secretaries from the surrounding movie studios got up like hookers, tourists, and a guy with no shirt and a completely tattooed chest and back depicting Japanese dragons. Phil Hanning was in back, half standing, motioning wildly to Zalman.

Zalman pushed through the mob to the table where Hanning was nibbling at a plate awash with herring. Hanning was a big, bluff man with blue eyes that crinkled when he smiled, regular features, blond wavy hair, and lots of even white teeth. He was dressed in silver Mylar sweat pants with many fancy zippers and a T-shirt which had the word "Bland" emblazoned across the chest.

"Zally," he said happily, herring juice dribbling out of the corner of his mouth.

"Jesus," Zalman moaned. He sank onto a plastic chair and motioned for the waitress, a hefty girl with a pile of hair on her head that looked like an orange bird's nest.

"What'll it be?" she asked around a wad of gum. "We got some nice herring."

"Jesus," Zalman said again. "Coffee, Alka-Seltzer, a heated Danish, plain, no fruit on it."

"Rough night?" The waitress grinned. She

snapped her order pad and sauntered off, her bird's nest bobbing through the throng.

"Phil," Zalman said, staring balefully at his brother-in-law, "if you don't tell me why I'm here within, oh, say, the next four seconds, I am going to ram that goddamn herring into your eyeballs." The waitress returned with his coffee and Alka-Seltzer, slopping both onto the table as she set them down. Zalman drank the Alka-Seltzer. "Four seconds, Phil," he said, belching slightly.

"I lost ten thousand bucks," Hanning said miserably.

"Lost? What lost?" Zalman said, sipping tepid coffee. "It fell out of your car while you were on your paper route? You left it in the dryer at the laundromat and some other guy took it home with his socks? Explain to me how you lose ten thou, Phil."

"Not that kind of lost, Jerry. I gave it to a guy and now he's gone."

"I'm shocked. You gave it to a guy and now he's gone. He needed the money to get his sister an operation and out of the goodness of your heart you made him a little loan 'cause he was short till payday."

"Jesus, Jerry, give me a break, willya?"

Zalman looked at Hanning in amazement. "Phil, I have known you for what, fifteen years now? I honestly don't think that during that time a single month has passed when I haven't given you a break. So what happened to the money?"

"You remember that guy you introduced me to the time we had breakfast here?" Hanning asked.

"The time you borrowed fifty bucks from me for cab fare which you were going to messenger over to me at my office the next morning and which needless to say I've never seen since?"

"Al Hix," Hanning said.

"Oh Jesus. Sticky Al Hix? You gave Sticky Al Hix ten thousand dollars? That's like asking a rat to hold your gouda." Zalman wadded up his paper napkin and threw it on the table. "Thanks for the Alka-Seltzer, Phil. My best to Lucille and good luck at your funeral." He started to stand up, but Hanning grabbed his coat and yanked him back down into his seat.

"Zally, I'm begging you. It'll be the last time, I swear. Just help me out here and I'll never come to you again, not for a nickel."

"Yeah, right," Zalman said flatly.

"Look," Hanning reasoned, "I gave him money before and everything worked out, so I figured . . ."

The table was covered with herring splashes, and Zalman took a napkin and wiped Hanning's place clean. "How about I tell you what happened, Phil?" he said. "Al Hix came to you and said he had some lovely jewelry. A little dubious, as it happened, so he was willing to let go of it at a reasonable cost, especially seeing as how you're my brother-in-law and all. You bought a necklace or some rings or maybe it was a fur coat, right?"

"Yeah," Hanning said. "It was a sapphire ring for Lucille. This time Al said he was going to buy a bunch of antiques, very high-priced stuff, and I figured I couldn't lose."

"Can't lose?" Zalman mocked. "Let me set you straight. There's no such animal as can't lose." The waitress arrived with his Danish and slopped some more coffee into his cup. "Thanks, darling," Zalman said tightly.

Hanning sat quietly, eyes pinned on the remnants of his decorative parsley. "He's done this before, hasn't he?"

"No more than three or four hundred times, I'd think," Zalman said. "It was Lucille's money?"

"Yeah," Hanning said a little too quickly.

Zalman knew he was lying. Lucille hadn't given Hanning more than fifty dollars at a time for years, ever since he'd lost a bundle buying desert land in Antelope Valley. Zalman let it pass.

"When was Al supposed to talk to you?" he asked tiredly.

Hanning brightened. "Last Wednesday."

"Now it's Sunday. Jesus, I don't know why I let you sucker me. Okay, I'll see what I can do, but I'm getting a little tired of picking up after you, Phil. Quit trying to be a wise guy. The role ill becomes you—you're just not a fast guy. A nice guy but not a fast guy."

Zalman pulled out his Gucci wallet, flipped a ten onto the table, and stood up. "Think about what I said, Phil, and maybe we can keep peace in the family. Talk to me later."

"Okay, Zally," Hanning said, flashing a toothy juvenile lead smile. "I'll do just what you tell me."

"Sure," Zalman mumbled as he threaded his way out of the Finest Snax. "Right."

11

ZALMAN DROVE HOME AND TOOK ANOTHER SHOWER. Tammy was gone and his cantilevered house in the Hollywood Hills was quiet and peaceful. He put on his new red spandex trunks and swam forty laps in his pool, then relaxed in a wrought-iron chaise lounge and scanned the Sunday edition of the *New York Times*. After that he watched some cable sports, but all that jumping made him tired and he took a nap on his cream linen living room sofa.

Still later that afternoon, as the desert shadows stretched out from the foothills, Zalman drove back to the Valley to look for Sticky Al Hix. He knew of course that there was almost no chance of recovering Hanning's ten thousand dollars, but it was probably Lucille's ten thousand and she was his only sister and besides, he was between divorces, his work load was depressingly routine, and he was bored.

Jerry Zalman had come a long way for a kid who'd been a quasi activist in the late sixties when he was studying prelaw at UCLA. Actually, his political activities weren't motivated by a crise de conscience but by his discovery that student rallies, draft-card burnings, and other such sports were a fabulous way for a short guy to pick up tall girls. Finally, however, the prospect of a tarnished future knocked some sense into his head and he dropped out of what he would later refer to as the "Kampus Follies" just before his best buddy, Doyle Dean McCoy, an Irishman with a great reverence for both whiskey and the IRA, kidnapped a college dean and held him hostage for a couple of hours. Afterward, McCoy transferred to San Quentin for two years and Zalman transferred to USC, where he made the dean's list. He always said that timing was everything.

Following law school he buzzed into the D.A.'s office and then into a prestigious downtown law firm where he quickly began to carry the ball on sensational and lucrative cases; then he'd gone out on his own, seeking and finding clients who made him rich and piqued his interest. But for some time now, ever since his second divorce, he'd felt boredom breathing heavily in his ear. Things were too simple. Blondes abounded. The clients were paying their bills with stunning regularity, cases rolled off his back with elegant simplicity, and life was settling into a groove that felt depressingly middle-aged.

Now Zalman nosed the Mercedes through Sunday traffic on Ventura Boulevard on his way to the Brass Rooster, a plush steak house where Sticky Al Hix sometimes drank his lunch and sold his slightly warm goods to the unwary. The drive took all of twenty-five minutes, during which Zalman played Vivaldi's *Four Seasons* on his tape deck and smoked a Cuban cigar.

When he arrived at the Rooster, Zalman saw he'd timed it right. It was four-thirty in the afternoon and things were slow. Billy, the heavily freckled head bartender, was mopping down the long mahogany bar and getting things ready for the evening.

"Jerry." He smiled as Zalman took a stool near the cash register. "How's the law biz?"

The two men shook hands over the bar. Like many people, Billy owed Zalman a debt of gratitude. Zalman had quietly taken care of his daughter's pot bust a few years back and had refused Billy's attempts to pay the debt. "Comp me," Zalman had told him, knowing he'd never pay for another drink in the Brass Rooster.

"Not bad, Billy." Zalman grinned. "Could be better, could be worse."

Billy nodded his graying head. *"Comme ci comme ça*, as they say."

"Hey, you went to high school?" Zalman laughed. "What a world. How about a Bullshot, pal?"

"You got it," Billy replied, freckles dancing over his face. "Hot?" Zalman nodded and Billy poured boiling water over a pair of bouillon cubes and stirred, then splashed in vodka. "So things are okay?" he asked again.

"Seen Al Hix around?" Zalman asked as he surveyed the long dining room where waiters were serving the few early diners. They were mostly oldsters who'd tripped in after a matinee for a hunk of steak before toddling home to the glitter stucco condos surrounding Ventura Boulevard.

Billy laughed. "You? Sticky Al burned you? Say it ain't so, pal. You're breaking my heart."

Zalman waved a mocking fist at Billy. "Gimme a break," he laughed, echoing Hanning's words. "I'm trying to find him for a friend. Seen him around?"

"Last week," Billy said, putting the Bullshot before Zalman. "He came in with a very nice-looking lady. Much too good for him, if you know what I mean. Short girl, about your height . . . Oh, Jesus, Jerry, I didn't mean that . . ." Billy was appalled by his own gaffe.

Zalman held up a placating hand. "A guy who is only five-five," he said magnanimously, giving himself the usual half inch, "is a short guy. He may be a rich guy. He may be a great guy. But he's a short guy. Go on, Billy. Tell me about the girl. Ever seen her in here before?"

"Yeah," Billy mumbled, fussing with Zalman's paper coaster. "She comes in lunchtime every so often, but I never seen her with Al before, if that's any use to you. Listen, hang on a second, I'll go ask Sandy. Maybe she knows where the girl works or something. I'm really sorry, man, no offense," Billy said, still feeling bad about his reference to Zalman's height. Billy opened the trap next to the service well and went to the front desk to talk to Sandy, the regular hostess. Zalman sipped his drink, watching them in the mirror over the back bar. Billy nodded and returned to his post behind the bar.

"Sandy says this girl runs a typing service, scripts and stuff, down the Boulevard somewhere. It's a run-down place that looks like a Western town setup. Sandy doesn't know her name, but if you keep your eye peeled you can't miss the joint. On the hill side of the street."

Zalman finished his Bullshot and laid a ten on the bar, but Billy protested and Zalman returned the bill to his wallet. "Adios, pal." He grinned. "Maybe I'll see you later."

"No offense?" Billy asked.

"No offense." Zalman grinned as he left. "None whatsoever."

Zalman got back in the Mercedes and pulled out into traffic, heading west down the Boulevard toward the girl's typing place. "I'm on a fooool's errand," he sang in deep operatic tones, "a fooool's errand." He cruised slowly down the broad street and watched the Wellington palms sway in the late-afternoon smog. Sunday strollers were admiring storefronts filled with gourmet cookware and marked-down jeans. Seniors were walking fat little dogs. Kids were whipping down the sidewalks on skateboards. It was pleasant and peaceful. It was well-heeled America on Sunday afternoon.

A few minutes later he found the place, parked the Mercedes, and jogged across four lanes of lazy traffic to the other side of the street. As Sandy said, Marie's Typeit was one of several shops housed in a low, rambling building with a false Western front, half done in weathered boards, the rest finished off in plywood covered with chipped paint. Typeit was sandwiched between a forward-your-mail joint and a pair of painted-over plate glass display windows that looked like they concealed fifty Asian women hunched over Singers, turning out Vuitton knock-offs.

The door to Typeit was standing open, and as Zalman walked up the driveway he was suddenly aware of the noise his leather soles made as they crunched the weed-infested gravel that passed for landscaping. Ahead in the cool shadows he heard the clack of a typewriter. He stuck his head inside the open door. There was no one in view, but from a back room the clatter of typing continued. Then he heard something else. Someone was singing a solid amateur version of "Blue Moon."

It was a strong voice, untrained but very nice nonetheless. It rose and fell with feminine intensity above the clatter of the electric typewriter.

Zalman stepped into the little front office and leaned against the composition-board counter. "I hate to interrupt," he called. "Hello?"

The singing stopped abruptly and a chair shrieked on the floor. A short girl with curly reddish hair and a delicate round face poked her head through the door from the back room. Dark eyes sized him up coolly. "We're closed," she said in a voice that had just a tinge of huskiness to it. It was the same voice that had been singing a moment earlier.

"I need something in a hurry," Zalman said, smiling encouragingly. "It won't take long, I promise." He gave her his A-1-sterling-fellow look. It usually worked.

She stared at him, noting his tailor-made shirt, his blue linen blazer, his gold Piaget watch, and his fifty-dollar haircut. "I warn you," she said, "I charge triple time for rush orders."

"And worth every dollar, I'm sure." Zalman smiled back.

Her brown eyes swept him once again, deciding. "Okay, I need a break anyway. Be right with you." She disappeared and a second later he heard the sound of running water; then she was back, drying her red-nailed hands on a paper towel, which gave Zalman a chance to check her out.

She was wearing a rose-colored T-shirt over her considerable chest; tight, faded jeans; and small diamond stud earrings. She looked pretty normal, he decided, except that she was wearing an old Spiro Agnew watch. She had a straight little nose, full little lips, and a thick mane of shoulder-length auburn curls. The face wasn't exactly a thing of beauty, but it held a strong allure all the same. Zalman noted something else when she looked at him over the counter, eyeball to eyeball. He saw that she was exactly his height. He cleared his throat. "I'm Jerry Zalman, Miss . . ."

"Marie," she said. "What can I do for you?"

"What do you usually do?" Zalman asked, leaning forward on the counter.

Marie cocked her head. Her hand slid slowly under the counter and Zalman had an uncomfortable feeling that it was going to come up full of something unpleasant.

"Hey." He laughed heartily. "You got me wrong."

"Oh, I don't think so," she said evenly. Her hand remained under the counter. "Why don't you tell me what you want?" she suggested, and Zalman saw she wasn't scared of him, not one bit. He liked that.

"Okay, okay. Pure and simple. I'm looking for Al Hix. Seen him around?"

"Who sent you?" she demanded in a voice that had become chilly.

Zalman decided to switch tactics and try the assertive approach. "Look, dear," he countered. "This isn't a federal case. I just want to find Al. I owe him some money."

To his surprise she burst out laughing. "Right," she said. "You owe him some money from last payday and thought you'd be a sport on Sunday afternoon and run around looking for him so he could get some medicine for his sick mother." Her hand came up from under the counter, and sure enough it held a snub-nosed Colt .38 Detective Special.

Zalman felt a lazy smile spread across his face. The day was moving right along. "Say," he told her brightly, "you're all right. A little short for my taste but you're all right."

She gave him a blank stare, then shook her auburn hair. "This is unbelievable. You think this is a Bogart movie or what?"

Zalman grinned and twitched his lip. "Yeah, sweetheart," he said. He let a few seconds tick by, then settled a look of sheer horror on his face as he looked over her shoulder. "Hey!" he barked. She didn't exactly fall for the old gag but it rattled her concentration for a split second, and that was all Zalman needed to lunge forward and jerk the gun neatly out of her hand.

"No, dear," he said. "I don't think this is a movie, but I do think you should have shot me. If I am the depraved killer you think I am then you are now about to become dead meat. If on the other hand I am a nice guy then everything's jake, as the girl said to the sailor."

"Creep," she murmured, rubbing her wrist. "Who are you?"

"Doghouse Riley, the man who didn't grow very tall."

"*The Big Sleep*," she said sulkily. "So what?"

"Very good," he said. "Like I said, I'm looking for Al Hix. I'm an attorney. You were right about one thing, though. I do not owe him money. He owes my brother-in-law money."

"This is ridiculous," she said, eyeing her gun, which Zalman still held by the short barrel. "Now what?"

Zalman smiled. Despite her height she was

very pretty. "Maybe you'd make me a cup of coffee and tell me the whole sad story about how Al promised you the moon."

"Al Hix," she shot back, "is not my boy-friend!"

"Okay, okay. Do you have a boyfriend or are you married?"

"What's it to you?" she asked, her voice rising.

"Unmarried, I take it. How about that coffee?"

She stared at him blankly, then turned and went into the back room. "I'll tell you one thing," she said over her shoulder. "I wish I'd stayed in bed this morning."

"You're not the only one," Zalman said, think-ing briefly of Tammy. He slipped the .38 into his jacket pocket, hoping it wouldn't stretch the material, and followed her back. As he did he realized she was wearing three-inch heels. *My God*, he thought. *She's shorter than I am.*

The big back room was filled with a half dozen battered desks, each one topped with a mighty IBM electric. Composition-board bookcases along one wall held reams of wrapped typing paper, and there was a huge Xerox machine opposite. A small refrigerator, a hot plate, and a chipped Formica lunch table took up another wall. There was a lavatory farther back beside a steel-sheathed alley door. The big workroom was flooded with fluorescent light from ceiling fix-tures. It looked like a place where people worked long, hard hours under pressure.

"You don't do all the typing yourself, do you?" he asked.

She gave him an appraising glance. "I have three regulars and I hire extra women when I need them. I'm going to computerize soon.

These things," she said, nodding at the IBMs, "are the washboards of the eighties."

Zalman laughed. She gave him a minuscule smile, then turned and headed back to the hot plate to mix a dose of hot water and Yuban. She had a very nice figure, he observed, very fully packed. Not too skinny or muscular like a lot of girls.

"Look, I'm sorry about the gun," she said as she handed him a mug. "I just got paranoid, you know? This woman across the street got raped last week so I got the gun."

"You just got this gun? You ever fired a gun?" She shook her head. "Jesus," Zalman said. "If I'd realized you didn't know how to use it I wouldn't have grabbed it off you. Don't ever let anybody take a gun off you. Kill 'em. Never mind the liberal limousine crap. Just nix 'em."

She grinned. "Okay, Mr. Attorney. Next time somebody tries to take my gun away I'll kill 'em."

Zalman took the gun out of his pocket and hefted it in his hand. "Where does Al live?"

"He's been sleeping in his office next door, poor guy, ever since his wife threw him out. They had a place out in Thousand Oaks, I think. But he hasn't been around in a few weeks. I've been picking up his mail for him."

"Ahhh," Zalman said, smiling. "Now we're getting somewhere. So you have keys to his office perhaps?"

"Well, yeah," she said. "But you can't—"

"Why can't I?" Zalman asked. "Tell you what. I'll trade you your gun back for the keys." He grinned at her.

She studied him for a moment, then laughed,

opened her desk drawer, and pulled out two old-fashioned embossed Master Lock keys strung on a rubber band. "I must be nuts. First I pull a gun on you. Now I hand over Al's keys, and I don't even know who you are."

"Never mind the self-doubt. Hand over the keys."

She gave him the keys and he gave her the pistol, which she put away in the desk drawer. "Come on, good-looking." He leered like Groucho. "How about a little breaking and entering?"

Marie laughed like she meant it, and the tension went out of her face. She didn't giggle and cover her mouth like a Japanese business-man. She really threw back her head and let it out, affording him a glimpse of pearly little teeth and a pink tongue.

"Now it's breaking and entering," she said. "What's next, Mr. Attorney?"

"I've got a good idea," he told her hoarsely, "but I'm repressing it." Marie shot him a ques-tioning look, but the smile didn't leave her lips. "Come on," he said quickly. "Maybe my brother-in-law's money is lying around on the floor, and then we can go for Chinese food."

"Okay," she said, glancing at him through lowered lashes. "You can ply me with liquor and tell me how you took the first step on the road to ruin."

"Careful. I'm a Sunday school lad."

Marie arched her delicate eyebrows and led him out of her office to Sticky Al's cubbyhole around the corner and down a little pathway thick with crabgrass and throw-away newspa-pers. The plate glass window that comprised the front wall was painted over, and there were more wind-ripped, yellowing papers on the rubber welcome mat.

"What did Al use this place for?" Zalman wondered aloud as he inserted the key in the corroded lock.

"Always sticks," Marie said. "Wiggle it around." Zalman glanced at her, then jiggled the key until the tumblers clicked. "Maybe that's why they called him Sticky Al," she said as he opened the door.

Al's office was dark, cool, and smelled of stale air and mildew. The painted window suffused the room with an aqua glow, and Zalman flicked on the ceiling light. The room held a scarred wooden desk in one corner, a studio couch with a cheap brocade cover, and a pile of crinkled paperback thrillers stacked beside it on the dirty linoleum floor. A soiled Izod polo shirt hung from the back of a fake oak desk chair, and there were a couple of polyester Hawaiian sports shirts hanging in a cubbyhole closet with no curtain.

"He was camping out here all right," Zalman said as he went through the desk drawers, which were empty except for some cheap toiletries and a few office supplies. "Poor old Al. The guy didn't even have a phone. I should have bought more stuff from him. A guy shouldn't have to live like this in today's world."

"You're spoiled," Marie said. "You know that?"

"I am," he admitted frankly. "But I've worked hard for it, and I intend to stay that way. What's in there?" he asked, nodding toward a closed door even as his hand reached for the greasy knob.

"Kitchen-bath."

Zalman opened the door, poked his head inside, and took a look around.

"Find what you're looking for?" Marie taunted.

The room was surprisingly large in comparison to the cramped bedroom-office. There was a very big, old-fashioned Frigidaire humming next to the back door. A tin shower stall with a wall sink next to it stood in one corner. Beyond that lay an alcove with a cheery flowered curtain hiding the toilet. An enamel-topped kitchen table had been shoved under a big window that looked onto a vacant lot with a little lemon tree standing in the center. In the fading afternoon light the tree was startlingly green, as if it drew nourishment from a secret water source known only to itself.

Zalman noted two mugs of coffee standing on the table, one partly empty, the other full. "Al had company, but it looks like someone didn't have time to finish," he said. The tree and the girl and the oncoming dusk made him suddenly sleepy. He looked out the window again, admiring the unexpected pastoral effect in the midst of the city's gigantic concrete madness.

Marie pushed past him and looked around. "I'll bet he left milk in the fridge," she said to herself. "I ought to dump it before it turns into a science project."

Zalman heard the click of the Frigidaire's door, then her strangled cry. As he wheeled and moved instinctively toward her she was grappling with a man who seemed to have leapt from the refrigerator. The man dragged her down to the floor and Zalman grabbed him, tearing him off the girl. As his hands clawed at the limp form

24

he realized with a shudder that he'd found Sticky Al Hix.

Zalman yanked the dead body onto its side as Marie moaned. "Oh no, oh no, oh God!" She rubbed her arms furiously as if she could erase the dark and ugly touch of death. Al wasn't icy, Zalman noted with the lawyerly, detached part of his mind. It . . . he hadn't been in the refrigerator very long.

He reached for Marie, but she came alive and scuttled backwards on the floor, jammed herself into a corner, and hunched there as a series of spasms rocked her. "Oh Jesus," she gasped. "What's going on?"

"Isn't that my line?" Zalman said through a painfully dry throat. He wrapped a handkerchief around his hand, then forced himself to go through the pockets of Sticky Al's khaki jump suit. There was a dirty blue canvas wallet with a Velcro snap, but it didn't contain much: several credit cards in various names, a driver's license with a crossed-out address in Thousand Oaks, a dry-cleaning ticket, and three dollars in neatly folded bills. There was no trace of Phil Hanning's ten thousand.

Zalman found his pocket notebook and wrote down the address in Thousand Oaks, then replaced the wallet. Still using the handkerchief-wrapped hand he probed Al's other pockets, but except for some loose change, a crumpled pack of Kools, a gnawed Bic lighter, and a key ring, they offered up nothing but cold lint. Zalman put his handkerchief away, satisfied he hadn't left his fingerprints anywhere, then looked around the kitchen. Nothing had changed except that the light through the back window had grown duskier. Nothing had changed except that Sticky Al Hix had hustled his last tawdry trinket. There was only one thing wrong. Hustling suckers with hot jewelry or antiques wasn't usually a killing offense, even in the roughest social circles.

Zalman extended a hand to Marie, still huddled in the corner. "Come on, cutie, you can get up now."

She didn't move. "You're a maniac!" she spat. "I wish I *had* shot you!"

"No, you don't want to kill me," he said smoothly, trying to recover his aplomb. "You didn't kill old Al here by any chance?" He said it fast to gauge her reaction.

"What!" she sputtered, outraged. She frowned and made an obvious effort to get hold of herself. "No," she said in a controlled voice. "And you didn't either, I suppose?"

"Just a squeaky clean bystander."

She sighed heavily, then stood up, her tense shoulders dropping. She tried not to stare at the body. "So who did?" she asked slowly in a tired voice.

"Exactly my question, toots," Zalman thought out loud. "And why am I here?" His shoulders slumped under the well-tailored padding of his jacket.

"I need a drink," Marie said flatly. "Then I am definitely calling the cops."

"As an officer of the court, I concur," Zalman said. "Unless of course you have something to hide."

"You're a riot. I've known you ten minutes and I can tell you're a real riot," she told him. She turned and marched out of the room.

"Just testing," he called after her, then followed her out of Al's cubbyhole and up the path to Typeit.

He found her in the back room, rummaging around in the bottom drawer of one of the desks. "Ha!" she exclaimed as she pulled out a grimy-looking bottle of generic scotch containing about a quarter of a fifth. "Linda keeps this around for emergencies and this is definitely one of 'em." She wiped the neck of the bottle with a Kleenex, took a ladylike swig, and made a nasty face. "Want some?"

Zalman took the bottle and inspected the label with horror. "I'll tell you one thing," he said. "If I'm taking you to the church social next week you'll have to upgrade your taste in scotch, coffee, and probably start wearing silk underwear." He sniffed the bottle and shuddered. It smelled like diesel.

Marie glared at him, then cradled the phone receiver on her shoulder and dialed. "Homicide, please," she told someone at the other end of the wire. "Captain Thrasher."

Suddenly, Zalman got a very bad feeling in his stomach. "Hey," he said slowly. "What's going—"

"Hello, Daddy, it's me," Marie said primly. "Something really terrible just happened . . ."

Zalman decided he'd have that drink after all.

Detective Captain Arnold Thrasher and Jerry Zalman went back a long way, all the way back to the days when Zalman was trying to pick up tall blondes on the antiwar picket line at UCLA and Thrasher, still a patrolman, was known as the Radical's Curse. He'd been the cop most likely to accidentally kick you in the crotch while helping you out of the dean's office, the cop who'd probably bruise your skull the hardest while assisting you into the back of the patrol car, the cop most likely to give you a taste of mace.

Indeed, it had been Thrasher who'd captured Zalman's pal Doyle Dean McCoy for no damn reason at all, according to McCoy, except that McCoy had kidnapped one of the deans and was holding him hostage in a utility closet when Thrasher caught up with them. It had largely been on Thrasher's fulsome testimony that McCoy had gone to San Q.

It had been fifteen years, but Thrasher recognized Zalman right off. "You shrimp son of a bitch," Thrasher roared as he stormed into Marie's office. "What have you done to my little girl?"

Unlike his daughter, the captain was six-three and weighed around two-fifty. He had grizzled iron-gray hair clipped Marine style and a fleshy, blue-jawed face. The walnut butt of his big .357 Magnum pistol peered around the edge of a gray drip-dry suit that looked like it had languished in the dryer for three or four years before Thrasher put it on. A blue polyester tie decorated with lobsters and regulation thick-soled cop shoes completed his ensemble.

"Nice to see you too, Arnie," Zalman said as he reached into his jacket pocket for his card, just to show Thrasher he was a respectable lawyer now and not a campus heckler. "Pity we had to meet again under these unhappy circumstances." He gave Thrasher the card and said nothing else. One of the most important things a man in Zalman's dodge had to know was when to keep quiet, and this was one of those times.

Thrasher took the card in one hand, scanned it, then jammed it in a pocket. His other arm was wrapped around Marie with proud solicitude, and Zalman was astonished at the ease with which she regressed into the role of daddy's little darling, her eyes misting over with Disney tears. Not for Captain Arnold Thrasher were the ways of the modern father. No laissez-faire permissive go-ahead-and-smoke-it parenting for him. Never mind that his little girl was twenty-seven or -eight—she was still his little girl. As soon as Thrasher satisfied himself that Marie was in one piece he bowed slightly in an "after you, Alphonse" gesture and ushered Zalman out the door.

Zalman led the captain and two plainclothesmen up the pathway to the other office. Sticky Al lay right where Zalman and Marie had left him on the green linoleum floor. Thrasher shot Zalman a look as sharp as a welding torch, and the two silent detectives took up positions on either side of the kitchen door. Thrasher knelt down ponderously and looked the body over carefully, barely touching it except to flick the collar of Al's jump suit with a ballpoint pen, just enough to check for the absent pulse in his scrawny blue neck.

The big cop breathed heavily through his pitted nostrils as he went about his grim work, and Zalman was surprised by his unexpected gentleness toward the dead. His slow movements suggested a lifetime of studying victims and a corresponding attitude of pity toward them. Finally he hoisted himself upright and brushed imaginary dust motes from the knees of his wash-and-wears.

"Well, well." He exhaled through his teeth,

regarding Zalman through icy eyes that gave away nothing. "So you're an attorney now? That must be interesting work. He a client of yours?"

Zalman smiled and cleared his throat. "A client of mine was looking for Mr. Hix. Miss Thrasher thought he might be here. Mr. Hix had given her keys to his office to collect his mail. We came in and found him, in the refrigerator. Miss Thrasher thought Mr. Hix left milk in there and it might be going sour. That's why she opened the refrigerator."

Thrasher raked his hair with blunt fingernails. "Jesus. This for real? Somebody killed this guy and stuck him in the refrigerator? Poor jerk's been shot in the chest, by the way, but I suppose a sharp guy like you picked that up right off."

"No," Zalman said. "All I noticed was he was dead. Perhaps—"

"Yeah," Thrasher interrupted. "Perhaps somebody wanted to keep him nice and cold, or maybe he inflicted this wound on himself and hopped in there to take the swelling down, huh? Why me?" he asked the two silent cops rhetorically. "Why do I get the nut calls? Why not Hamburg or Reilly? Why are those guys always taking a leak when the nut calls come in?" he asked, forgetting that this particular nut call had come from his own daughter. The two cops cleverly maintained their silence.

Thrasher turned back to Zalman. "How come you were looking for Sticky Al?" he demanded.

Zalman took a deep breath. "I would be forced to say that a great deal of my relationship with

Mr. Hix falls between the pillars of privileged information."

"Why, sure it does, bless your heart," Thrasher said, beaming like a cobra. "Sit down, you shrimp son of a bitch, while I try and put you in the picture."

Zalman sighed and sat down.

SIX HOURS LATER ZALMAN RETURNED HOME TO his hot tub, his blue velvet sleep mask, his movie posters, his rows of three-piece suits hanging faithfully in his walk-in closet. His private world was still intact, mercifully untouched by the tense hours he'd spent with Captain Arnold Thrasher at the Van Nuys police station. Although Zalman had eventually given up Phil Hanning's name, address, social security number, and shirt size, he'd done it grudgingly, making Thrasher dig for it. A man in Zalman's line of work couldn't cave in too easily and, besides, he wanted Thrasher to understand he was an upscale citizen these days and not a nineteen-year-old pisher.

But it was obvious that the years hadn't mellowed Thrasher's opinion of Zalman one bit, nor did he believe Zalman's story about Hanning, the late Al Hix, or the late ten thousand. At least Zalman was spared one problem: Thrasher didn't know Zalman had technically tampered with evidence by rifling Al's pockets. Before the big cop hauled Zalman down to the Van Nuys station Al's body was searched and photographed by a police forensics team and removed by the coroner's men, but apparently Zalman's caution with the handkerchief had done the trick. Zalman was relieved. As an officer of the court he knew he should have kept his mitts out of Al's pockets, but as a realist he needed Al's address.

Zalman groaned as he peeled off his clothes, lit a cigar, and lowered himself gratefully into his bubbling hot tub, beside which he'd positioned a generous snifter of Courvoisier. The Dunhill clock clicked 2:00 A.M., but Zalman knew it was lying. It felt like the Thrasher family had held him in its talons for centuries. He leaned back on the tiles, let the sprightly water lap him with its comforting tickle, and tried to think.

He had a bad feeling and he didn't like it. He'd run into a mess he hadn't bargained for, a mess that promised to be way more than a diverting interlude between cases. Had Hanning set him up? Zalman couldn't believe it. He'd known his brother-in-law for fifteen years and knew that Hanning could barely make it into the express line at the Safeway, let alone plan a complicated frame. Still, it was a possibility that had to be considered. All possibilities were worth considering.

Zalman knew Thrasher hated his guts, and given half a chance the big cop would railroad him for Sticky Al's murder. Zalman hated to admit it, but it looked like he'd fumbled the ball on this one, and tired as he was he knew something else: if anybody was going to get him out of Thrasher's frame it would have to be himself. On that note, he dried off, put on his Pierre Cardin pajamas, and got into bed, hoping once again to encounter the peaceful but elusive village of his dreams.

* * *

At ten sharp the next morning Zalman, clad in a dark three-piece suit, arrived at his office in the penthouse of a five-decker building on Beverly Drive and started barking orders at his Eurasian secretary, Esther Wong. Esther, who was tall, beautiful, and dim in the cranial department, couldn't handle pressure, and after a few seconds Zalman lowered his voice. Over the years he'd made a lot of allowances for her because she dressed up the office with her cheongsams, her lustrous dark hair, and her Lucite smiles. On the other hand, she'd made allowances of her own for his churlish temper and erratic work habits, and overall he was forced to admit the relationship had proved solid.

"One," he snapped, "get my sister for me. Try the house. Get her out of the studio if necessary. Just get her."

"Mr. Z.," Esther tried to interrupt.

"Two, after I speak to Lucille, get that jerk brother-in-law of mine. I want him in the office before I see my sister, which I will do at lunch. Three, make a reservation for two at Le Croque, the little alcove room, so tell Pierre if somebody's got it already throw them the hell out." Swinging his Gucci briefcase Zalman headed for his private office.

"By the way," Esther called, doing her best to poke the buttons on the phone despite her two-inch red nails, "there's somebody in your office."

"And four," Zalman said, barging into his big office, "get McCoy on the horn. Who the hell are you?" he demanded as a tall, blond young man jumped up nervously from the deep leather couch.

"Chuck Downley," the blond man stammered,

34

clutching a copy of *Variety* in front of his shocking pink flamingoed shirt. The rest of his outfit consisted of yellow linen slacks and yellow shoes with pointed toes.

Zalman sat down behind his big Victorian partner's desk and reached for his cigar case. "And what can I do for you, Chuck, old sport?" he said, scanning the headlines in the newspapers which Esther laid out each morning.

"Well, for one thing," Downley said, taking a leather-upholstered chair in front of the desk, "you can tell that creep brother-in-law of yours to back off. Tell him if he comes around me or Lila I'll kill him. I mean it!" His voice rose angrily.

Zalman decided the headlines could wait. *Hanning again*, he thought grimly. "What's the problem, Chuck?" he said in his smoothest voice.

"He's insulting, that's what he is. He told me to eat shit and die!"

Zalman coughed down a laugh. "Not very polite, I'll admit, but not exactly a criminal offense either. Take it from the top, will you? What's this all about?"

A crafty look settled behind Downley's pale eyes. "I heard Al Hix is dead."

"That's true," Zalman said noncommittally.

"Did he tell you about the antiques?"

Zalman inclined his head knowingly.

"It's very simple," Downley gushed. "Lila heard on the news that Al died. He was supposed to bring her the money yesterday and he never showed up, so I called Phil and told him Lila said since Al didn't bring the money the deal's off."

"Go on," Zalman said smoothly.

35

"No auction, no antiques," Downley said. "Then Phil starts screaming at me and says Lila has reneged and he's going to sue. Then he tells me to eat shit and die! I told Lila and she said to come over and tell you to get Phil off our backs. Whatever . . ." He trailed off.

Zalman sighed. "Let me get this straight. Al was supposed to deliver some money?"

"Thirty thousand. But he didn't, so Lila says they're out."

"They were going to buy some antiques from Lila? Who's Lila, your wife?"

"Don't be bitchy," Downley said. "My half-sister, Lila Henderson. She owns a large collection of antiques she's going to auction off because she broke up with her boyfriend a few months ago and we have to move out of the house in Encino, so we're going to Carmel."

"What's all this got to do with Phil?"

"Well, Lila thought if she took in some partners in front it would guarantee her a large amount of cash, no matter how the auction does. But no cash, no partners, right?" Downley whined.

"And Phil was a partner?"

Downley nodded.

Zalman brooded a moment, blew a couple of perfect smoke rings, and watched them float away over Downley's head. Downley's information was another part of the story Hanning had conveniently forgotten to explain yesterday when he'd merely said he'd given Sticky Al money to buy some antiques. Now the deal was starting to sound a lot more complicated, and though Zalman badly wanted to know who else was a partner in Phil's wacky setup he didn't want to let Downley know how little he knew.

"Look, Chuck," Zalman said briskly. "I'll talk

to Phil, all right? I'll get him off your back and we'll work it out, okay? Don't worry. Leave it to me, and while you're at it leave a number with Esther where I can get hold of you." Zalman stood up. "Talk to me later." He stuck out his hand and Downley took it in both of his.

"I don't deserve that sort of talk," Downley said moodily, still holding Zalman's paw. "Promise you'll call."

"Pinky swear, Chuck, old sport."

"Thanks so much," Downley breathed. "Lila will be ever so." Downley turned and went into the outer office.

Zalman sighed, went to his wet bar, and put some water on to boil. It was a good morning for a drink, and by the time Esther had tracked down his sister Zalman was back at his desk, bathing his face in the warm steam of his Bullshot.

"Good morning, Lucille," Zalman said. "Have a pleasant evening, I trust?"

The voice that rasped out of the phone was the exact duplicate of Zalman's, given minor allowances for sex. Tone for tone, however, Lucille Zalman Hanning's voice sounded like the feminine version of her brother's. "Stinking, Jerry," she replied without hesitation. "And yourself?"

"Cops keep you up late?" he inquired innocently.

"Hah! Six or so. Jerry, what the hell's going on? Wait, let's not talk about this over the phone. I'm in the studio anyway. Bland wants to cut all the computer enhancement out of his new album and he's driving me nuts. I swear I'm going to kill his skinny English ass." Lucille was a heavy hitter in the record business and Bland was her brightest star.

"Hold on," Zalman said. "I have to check with Fu Manchu's daughter." Zalman put his hand over the receiver and called to Esther, who yelled back that he had reservations for lunch at Le Croque. "One o'clock at Le Croque," he told Lucille. "Be there or be square." The Zalman siblings hung up without further conversation and Zalman had time to finish his drink, his cigar, and the morning papers before Phil Hanning shuffled into the office forty minutes later with all the élan of a mutt on its way to the pound.

"Why—" Zalman smiled wolfishly— "is that Phil Hanning's sprightly tread I hear upon my office floor? Great to see you, pal. What brings you by?"

"Cut the comedy, Jerry," Hanning said, sinking into a deep armchair and picking morosely at his tennis shoes. "I was up all night with the cops. I'm in the shitter."

"You're damn right you are!" Zalman screamed at him in a well-rehearsed rendition of uncontrollable rage. "I could have been killed yesterday! Cement shoes, Philly! Dead! Gone! Cancelled!" Zalman waited a few seconds until he figured Hanning had been softened up enough, then dropped his voice. "Now, Philly, tell old Uncle Jerry what really happened, huh? Tell Unk what you did."

Hanning's handsome face was a mask of misery. "Tell you the truth, Zally, I don't know. Al said my ten would get me fifty off this antique thing. Now he's dead, the money's gone, and the antique lady says we're out of the deal."

"You and Al?" Zalman probed. "He was your partner?"

"Yeah," Hanning said dejectedly. "There was

38

a little more to it than I said yesterday. He was gonna get me in if I came up with the bucks, and then he'd take a piece of the action. I did my part, but now look what's happened. Maybe someone croaked him for the money. Anyway, that's what that guy Thrasher kept asking about."

"Guy like Al Hix, who can say what he was into," Zalman muttered absently, wondering what else Hanning hadn't told him. "It could have been a hundred different reasons: an old debt, a bad debt, too many broken promises —who knows? But what I want to know about right now is your love affair with Chuck Downley."

Hanning looked startled. "What about him?" he asked slyly.

"Don't play games with me, Philly!" Zalman yelled. "He was in my office this morning when I got in."

"That guy!" Hanning blurted. "He's the brother of the antique lady, but now he says I'm out of the deal just because Al never turned over the money, but how do I know that? Like you said, maybe Al's death had nothing to do with any of this. All I have is Downley's word."

"Jesus," Zalman moaned. "All you have is air is what I'm hearing."

"All I wanted to do was make a little dough, Zally," Hanning whined. "You know, get Lucille stuff without using her money. Is that so bad?"

As an attorney who'd listened to a lot of sad stories over the immense partner's desk it went against Zalman's grain to feel sorry for anybody, but he had to admit he'd always felt a little sorry for Hanning. Lucille was a tough piece of action who made a lot of money and knew how to throw it around. Sure, she gave Hanning plenty of pocket money, but Zalman knew he had a point. It was her money, her house, her cars, her everything. Hanning held the coat, and it looked like the mink was growing weighty.

"Phil," Zalman asked sweetly, "what else didn't you tell me yesterday?"

"Ah, nothing," Hanning said, rubbing at his Mylar-clad knees. Zalman wondered if he was lying again, but he also knew a guy could only cop to so much foolishness in any one go-round.

He decided to switch tactics to see if it would shake Phil up a little. "Well, okay, Al's gone. It's too bad, of course, but better him than you. My advice is go home and chalk it up to experience."

To his surprise, Hanning shot out of his chair. "No way!" he barked in a shrill voice. "Maybe you can afford to blow off ten grand, but it's different with me."

"Hey, this is serious," Zalman snapped. "Al's dead. Next time it could be good-bye Philly or good-bye Jerry. Also, now I'm tied in with a killing, and that doesn't do my reputation any good. I know a lot of guys think I'm drifty and sometimes it doesn't hurt to let them, but I'm telling you I'm one hundred percent legit. I pay parking tickets personally, understand? But we'll worry about that later. Our problem now is convincing Thrasher. He hates my guts from fifteen years ago, and it looks like we're going to be lucky to get out of this whole. You got that, Phil? You listening?"

Hanning nodded miserably. "I got it, Zally," he said in a hushed voice.

"Okay," Zalman continued in a milder tone. "Here's what you do. Go home, play with the kids, cook up one of your gourmet specialties. Don't talk to anyone about anything. If Thrasher shows up again or calls or sends a guy over, call me. You receiving me, Phil?"

Hanning waved a manicured hand impatiently. "I'm not so dumb, Zally."

"We'll let that pass for now," Zalman said, ushering Hanning past Esther to the elevator. "Talk to me later."

"Call waiting, Mr. Z.," Esther purred when Zalman returned to the office.

"Who is it, Esther?" Zalman coaxed. "Concentrate."

"Oh, a girl. She said you met yesterday."

"Keep trying McCoy till you get him," Zalman reminded as he strode back into his office. "Hello, hot stuff," he said into the phone. "How's the body biz?"

"Jesus!" Marie Thrasher's voice said angrily. "Don't you ever stop?"

"Don't abuse me." He laughed. "Wait till we're married. Besides, you think I've had a swell evening with your dear old dad grilling me like a steak? Just trying to keep our relationship lighter than air, doll." Zalman grinned and swung around in his swivel chair, admiring Beverly Drive through his picture window. From his vantage point five floors up he could see the beautiful kiddies shopping madly up and down the street. The rate of conspicuous consumption in Beverly Hills had never been greater.

"Try to be serious, will you?" Marie implored. "I'd like to talk to you, strictly business."

"You can't afford me." Zalman laughed. He listened carefully and thought he heard the controlled gnashing of teeth. "But I'll tell you what. Simply because I happen to be an all-around great guy I'll let you buy me dinner. Maybe if you ply me with a few drinks and a piece of fresh salmon with hollandaise or maybe lamb chops with a lovely béarnaise sauce I'll throw caution to the winds and give you some free legal advice. Oh, I'll hate myself in the morning, but anything for justice. Remember, though, no plain-wrap restaurants. Jerry Zalman has his pride."

"If I were your mother I would have drowned you at birth. Okay, smart ass, you're on for eight o'clock." She gave him an address in Studio City.

"You told your dad you want to talk to me?" he asked.

"Look, Mr. Attorney," she said finally. "There are some things a girl can't tell her father, know what I mean?"

"On that we agree completely," he purred and they hung up. Zalman laughed as he replaced the receiver. Gone was his funk of the previous evening. The day was definitely breaking his way.

TWO HOURS LATER ZALMAN MADE HIS WAY
through the crush of gorgeous guys and gals
jamming the bar at Le Croque, Hollywood's
snitziest watering hole. Pierre, the oily owner,
waved obsequiously when he saw Zalman and
undulated his way through the crowd. Zalman
accepted Pierre's cheek-kissing with good
grace.

"M'sieu Zalman," Pierre growled in Charles
Boyer's old accent. "You sistair, she is not hair
yet." He shrugged his thin shoulders in an unconscious parody of Gallic nonchalance. "Perhaps an aperitif at zee bar?" he suggested.

Zalman happened to know Pierre's real name
was Pete Marchetti. He hailed from Cleveland
and once upon a time had been involved in
major unpleasantness involving the IRS and a
charge of tax fraud. Zalman had been his attorney and had waived a portion of what would
otherwise have been an enormous fee in ex-
change for eternal free eats at Le Croque, which
was very California cuisine and very pricey.

"Sure, Pete," Zalman stage-whispered. *"La
plume de ma tante* to you, too."

Pierre's rat face contorted, but he recovered
quickly and ran a nervous hand over his patent

leather hair. "M'sieu Zalman, he makes zee little joke. Zee Bullshot, non?"

"Zee Bullshot, yes," Zalman replied as he seated himself at the bar next to a pair of gigantic blond beauties Pierre kept around to decorate the place. Pierre slapped his shoulder and slipped into the crowd like a beaver into a mill pond.

"Say!" Zalman addressed the taller of the two girls. "Didn't we meet at the symphony last year?" The girl collapsed in a fit of giggles, elbowing him heartily. Her friend was staring vacantly around the crowded room in an imitation of a Scavullo cover for *Cosmo*. Zalman immediately lost interest and tucked into his second Bullshot of the day.

He was halfway through it when Lucille appeared in the fern-studded foyer, flanked by her two debonair assistants, Biff and Dex. As Lucille charged through the room she scanned the crowd quickly, determined there was no one there more important than herself, then turned the full brunt of her attention on her brother.

"Zally," she said throatily, taking the stool beside him, "what's going on?" As befitted a top executive in the record business Lucille believed in direct action. She motioned for Biff and Dex to fade, and they took up positions near the end of the bar. Because they wore identical corn-silk haircuts and expensive Italian threads, Zalman always had trouble telling them apart. Lucille, who was dressed for success in a gray skirt, blue blazer, and a string of pearls that could have doubled for grapefruits, signaled the bartender. "Scotch," she commanded in her raspy voice. "Perrier chaser. I

44

don't usually drink at lunch but this is serious. Zally, what's with Phil?''

Zalman hesitated. Talking to Lucille about Hanning was like talking to a tigress about her cub. Hanning was her blind spot. She'd married him in college when he was a handsome drama student and she was a short girl who adored him and had no doubt he would quickly conquer the silver screen. After graduation they'd set up housekeeping in a cheap Hollywood apartment and Hanning began to look for work. Predictably he didn't find it. Aside from his kisser Hanning didn't have much to recommend him, and after a few bit parts in films and TV his acting career died on the vine.

Meanwhile, Lucille, who was holding down a job as a secretary in a large record company, took stock of things and decided to strike out on her own. Despite Hanning's extravagances she'd managed to save a few thousand dollars, and with traveler's checks in hand she flew to London, signed four acts, and flew home, fifty dollars remaining. She blew the last fifty on a lunch for a nervous young executive for a small record label and persuaded him to listen to tapes of her four groups. He ended up making a deal and from that point Lucille had steamrolled forward like General Patton on a good day. Currently she managed several groups, the biggest of which was called Bland after its founding teen, a Cockney of minimal IQ who was blessed with a cruel stare that impressionable young girls took for depth.

Although Lucille was known all over town as a very tough lady, she was soft for Hanning, and that was why Zalman was now twirling his pink silk La Croque cocktail napkin instead of replying to her question about Hanning. After all, there was a lot to consider. Lucille and Phil Hanning had three children, two boys and a girl, and Hanning took care of them. In addition he ran their huge house in Toluca Lake, did the shopping, most of the cooking, and actually, except for his insecurities, was well suited to househusbandry. He had Lucille to take care of, and unlike many female executives in town Lucille had a real home and family to return to at the end of the grueling day instead of an empty apartment.

"Come on," Lucille told her brother. "I'm starved. Let's eat and then you'll tell me what the hell's going on."

Zalman ushered his sister through the sea of gnashing teeth to the white-lattice, beferned gazebo Pierre had reserved for them and seated himself with his back to the wall. Lucille sat next to him so she could also view the diners. "Me for some steak tartare," Zalman said as he scanned the leather-bound menu.

"Steak tartare for the gentleman," Lucille told the waiter. "I'll have smoked salmon, cold asparagus with the hollandaise on the side. Perrier with my meal."

Zalman shook his head and grinned. "You're so forceful, Luce," he teased.

"Puh-lease," she groaned. "I'm just trying to keep my head above water. Look now, Zally. This is bad, huh? Who's this Thrasher guy and what's he want with Phil? I mean, the kids want to know why Joe Friday's talking to their dad in the living room until six this morning." Her dark eyes stared anxiously at her brother, hoping to read good news on his face.

"Calm down," Zalman said. "We're all busy men or we wouldn't be here, right?" He proceeded to tell her the little he knew about Hanning, the missing ten thousand, Sticky Al Hix's murder, Thrasher, Chuck Downley, and the hard-luck antique deal. "Now, Lucille," he concluded, "speak to me as a wife. Did you give Phil ten grand?"

Lucille broke into hysterical laughter. "Phil?" she screeched. "Never in life! I love him. He's a great father and a terrific cook but that much cash . . ." She let it hang in the air conditioning as she frowned impatiently. "Honestly, I don't understand men. Why doesn't he leave it alone? Let me make the money, which is what I'm good at. Let him take care of the kids and house, which is what he's good at. What's the damned problem?"

Zalman nodded agreement as he forked a tad of salmon off his sister's plate. "He's got an ego is the problem. Jeez, this salmon is good. Make sure to mention it to Pierre so he won't be tempted to buy any cut-rate stuff. Okay, I didn't believe Phil's story about the money either."

"Oh God, where'd he get it?" Lucille moaned. "You think he stole it?" She put her hand on his. "Zally, you gotta find out about this, huh? Please, Zally?"

"Don't drive yourself nuts, Lucille," he said, downplaying the situation a little. "I'm already working on it."

"The thing about Phil," she said a minute later, "is he's really a good husband, in a very old-fashioned way. And even though I don't act like it I'm really a very old-fashioned girl."

"Don't worry, Luce," Zalman reassured. "I'll save your little garden of delight."

After lunch Zalman drove back to his office, where Esther told him she'd finally located Doyle Dean McCoy, Zalman's old school chum, who now ran a guard dog service and did errands for Zalman when things were slow. McCoy would be in soon. Zalman was washing up in his private bathroom off his office when he heard the sound of barking and Esther squealing, "Get him off me! You filthy thing!"

Zalman went to his office door and saw McCoy pulling a huge, sleek black Doberman away from Esther, who was trying to hide behind her swivel chair. "One of your highly trained guard dogs, I presume?" Zalman asked innocently.

McCoy grinned and shrugged and finally picked up the Doberman under one arm. "Say hello to the nice lawyer, Rutherford," he said, waggling one of Rutherford's paws at Zalman. He carried the dog into the inner office. "Yeah, old Ruth here had himself an easy gig patrolling a construction site out in Culver City, but he had to go and nip a cute lady architect in the posterior. Didn't you, Ruth, old buddy? So it looks like his guarding days are over, for a while anyway." McCoy shook his big head and dropped the dog on Zalman's carpet.

Zalman shut the door while McCoy helped himself to a bottle of beer from Zalman's fridge. He was twice Zalman's weight and a foot taller, a big, slow man with a creased face and shaggy brown hair. He was wearing jeans, a T-shirt, and snakeskin cowboy boots, and he was smoking an unfiltered Lucky Strike.

"You shouldn't smoke those," Zalman admonished for the umpteenth time. "They'll kill you."

"So what?" McCoy demanded, sprawling out on the deep couch. "I'm gonna die anyway. Might as well go happy. What's the problem, Jerry? Esther was doing her inscrutable bit and wouldn't give an inch." Rutherford made himself comfortable beside his master and McCoy gave him a sip of beer, then drank from the bottle himself.

Zalman shook his head and tried not to think about germs. He sat down behind his desk and lit a cigar. "You remember Arnold Thrasher?"

"That pus-brain? You bet your ass I remember him! I wouldn't have gone to the crossbar hotel except for old Arnie. Don't tell me he turned up again?"

"Please pay attention," Zalman said, "because I doubt if I can go through this twice. Yesterday Phil Hanning, whom you will remember, tells me he gave ten grand to Sticky Al Hix and, big surprise, now Al's nowhere to be found. I go to look for Al, who it develops has a fleabag office on Ventura Boulevard, right next door to a very pretty girl who does typing. Turns out she has keys to Al's office, so we go in and find Al jammed in the fridge, doing an imitation of a very dead mackerel. But the worst part is the girl happens to be Arnie Thrasher's daughter. Arnie, by the way, is now a homicide detective, a captain no less."

McCoy's big face broke into a wide grin and he started to laugh. "You want my advice, Jerry? Think about Tahiti or Australia or someplace out of the way like that. Oh boy!" he hooted. "Arnie Thrasher's daughter! I'm sure glad it happened to you, Jerry, and not me, 'cause I'd be dead already. Arnie would've carved me up into Alpo by now." He got up and fetched himself another beer.

"This morning," Zalman continued, ignoring McCoy's hooting, "a guy named Chuck Downley shows up in my office and says Al and Phil were supposed to give his sister, one Lila Henderson, a down payment to buy into a supposed antique auction this Henderson is running. Phil claims he got the money from Lucille, Lucille says he didn't, and I want to know where he really did get it. Also, I want to know who killed Sticky Al since if I don't find out before Arnie Thrasher gets nervous about his daughter being involved in a homicide, I know and you know Arnie's going to try and pin it on me. So the first thing I want you to do is find Mrs. Al."

Zalman scribbled down the address in Thousand Oaks he'd taken from Al's driver's license yesterday and passed the slip to McCoy. McCoy gave Rutherford another slug of beer, then drained the bottle and belched slightly. "Didn't know Al had an old lady," he said. "What about the auction deal?"

"I'll check into that myself. Run out to Mrs. Al's this afternoon, before I feel Thrasher's fetid breath on my neck. God, I hate that guy."

"Yeah," McCoy said dreamily. "I remember one time I was on the picket line at UCLA and Thrasher was there and—"

"Please, McCoy." Zalman groaned. "This is no time for fond memories. Try and hustle me up something. Mrs. Al is the only lead I've got."

"Okay, chief," McCoy said as he helped himself to another beer. "Usual rate?"

"Of course, of course! Only don't disappear for

a week or no dough! I'll check with you at the Compound later." The Compound was McCoy's place in Newhall, two acres of rocky hillside with a large mobile home on it and some kennels for the guard dogs he rented out to the unwary.

McCoy saluted and whistled to Rutherford, who burped and lay down on the floor. "Come on, you gink," he said to the dog. Rutherford whined piteously and rubbed his slobbery snout on Zalman's nice clean chair, leaving a sticky trail of drool.

"McCoy, give the upholstery a break, will you? You know what it costs to get a chair recovered these days?" Zalman wadded up a piece of paper and threw it feebly at Rutherford.

McCoy bent down and picked the dog up, cradling the Doberman like a baby. "Yowsah, yowsah, yowsah, Mr. Zalman," he rasped. "C'mon, Ruth, let's take off for tall timber." He pulled open Zalman's office door and stood face to face with Captain Arnold Thrasher. "Arnie!" he exclaimed. "What a goddamn pleasure to see you after all these years!" Rutherford gave a low growl and flattened his ears.

"I'd like to put a bullet through your lame brain, McCoy," the big cop said pleasantly. "Maybe if I worked at it I could get you and that ugly mutt with one shot."

"Boys, boys," Zalman said heartily. "I know you two are thrilled to see each other but try to contain your excitement, will you? McCoy, great to see you, buddy, drop by anytime you're cruising Beverly Hills. Arnie, a drink maybe, just to get the day rolling?"

Thrasher shot an ugly glance back and forth between Zalman and McCoy. "Don't call me Arnie," he said as he brushed past McCoy and settled moodily in an armchair. "Why the hell did they let you out of San Q, McCoy?" he asked petulantly. "I was hoping maybe you'd try to escape and they'd shoot you."

McCoy stared at the back of Thrasher's head. "Nice to see you too, Arnie, you old reptile." He waggled one of Rutherford's paws at Thrasher. "Hasta la boogie."

Zalman leapt forward and slammed his office door shut behind McCoy before he could come up with any more smart cracks. "So, Arnie, how about that drink?" he asked.

Thrasher shifted his bulk in the armchair. "Not while I'm on duty, *Mr.* Zalman." He looked slowly around Zalman's luxuriously appointed office, his eyes flicking over the furniture, the rugs, the pictures without missing a dust mote. "Nice setup you got here. Very expensive stuff, huh? You come by any of this dough honestly?"

Zalman ignored him and poured himself a Perrier. "The law is a demanding profession, but a well-paid one," he said sententiously.

Thrasher snorted derisively. "Now listen up, *Mr.* Zalman. You and that buggy friend of yours used to cause me plenty of trouble when you were a pair of pishers and I was a cop on the beat, but me, I'm a guy who'd be willing to let bygones be bygones—"

"Nice phrase—is it original?"

"—but now, all of a sudden, you two Bobbsey Twins show up again, and when my little girl is involved, well, lemme tell you, *Mr.* Goddamn Zalman, you get in my way and you'll wake up dead. You hear me? That's my little girl and I ain't kidding." Thrasher's voice was low and he spoke slowly and distinctly, without the malice that had tinged his voice when he'd spoken to McCoy. "Maybe you killed Hix, maybe not. But if you got dirty hands, I'm the guy to wash 'em for you. Get it? But stay away from Marie. That ain't a cop talking, that's a father. Get it?"

Zalman sipped his Perrier. "Arnie, Arnie, Arnie," he said softly. "Look around you. I work hard for the money. Every day I get up, I come into the office, I listen to my clients' problems, I try to help them. That's how I make my living."

"You're a regular Mother Teresa, aren't you."

Zalman ignored him. "I knew Sticky Al, sure. He's an around guy, but hey, he's strictly from hunger, right? Why would a guy like me blow off a great lifestyle for a guy like him?"

Thrasher glared at him malevolently. "I don't care, Zalman. I don't care who you are, what you do. I don't care about you and I don't care about Sticky Al Hix. I care about my daughter, and if you get in my way you won't be there long." Thrasher got up and thudded toward the door. He waved an admonitory finger at Zalman. "Get it?"

"Got it."

"Good." Thrasher slammed the door behind him.

Zalman resisted the urge to hurl his glass of Perrier at the closed door and settled for beating his clenched fists on his desk instead. What was a guy to do?

Zalman had some time to kill until he was to meet Marie Thrasher for dinner, so he drove out to Saks in the Valley to look for black silk socks with clocks on them. He'd wanted the socks ever since he'd seen Brian Donlevy wear them in *The*

Glass Key, and even though Alan Ladd thought they didn't show class Zalman sided with Brian Donlevy. Saks didn't carry them so he had a Häagen-Dazs instead, bought a bottle of Pouilly-Fuissé, and strolled around watching young Valley housewives flirting with handsome strangers prowling the mall. No wonder he did such a brisk divorce business, Zalman thought. There wasn't a husband in sight, only wives and lovers.

At five to eight Zalman pulled up in front of a small Spanish-style house on a quiet side street in Studio City. The house probably cost five thousand when it was built in 1938, but Zalman knew today you couldn't touch it for less than one-fifty. As he walked up the curling flagstone path to the front door he noted the house and fair-sized front yard were well tended. There were fuchsias and bougainvillea, the beds beneath the shrubberies were raked and clean, and there were dwarf lemon trees in bright ceramic urns beside the tiled doorway.

Zalman rapped on the oak front door, and when the girl didn't answer he tried the door and found it unlocked. He pushed it open and stuck his head inside. "Hello, Marie," he called. "It's a burglar. Can I come in?" He heard singing coming from the general direction of the kitchen.

Could he be hearing the theme song from "Gilligan's Island"?

"Very nice," Zalman called. "Try taking it down a tone, will you?" He closed the door behind him and looked around, seized with the weird feeling he'd stumbled into the middle of F.A.O. Schwarz. The living room was jammed with toys of all descriptions. In one corner there was a six-foot wooden Indian flanked by a carrousel horse and a plaster giraffe with a four-foot neck. A large set of mirrored shelves ran the length of the room and were lined with smaller toys: a mechanical bank, a tin zeppelin circling a tin Empire State Building, a yellow tin aquarium, tin soldiers, tin automobiles, tin farm animals. There was an odd-looking set of jointed wooden circus animals. There was a shelf filled with little rubber animals: dogs, cats, pigs, horses, an ostrich. One wall held a huge framed poster with the word "JUMBO!" on it and a picture of two little kids on an outsize elephant's back. The effect was humorous, yet clearly demented.

Interspersed with the mélange of toys was a 1950s black brocade sofa, a tomato-soup-colored plastic kidney coffee table, blond wood end tables, and easy chairs with bright canvas cushions. The windows were flanked by gardenia print draperies, and lighting was provided by several bullet-shaped lamps on floor pedestals. The furniture looked like it came straight from Dagwood Bumstead's living room.

"Oh, hi," Marie said, appearing in the arched doorway, drying her hands on an old-fashioned apron with a magenta flower pattern. Her hair was swept off her neck and fastened with a big rhinestone barrette. She wore purple sequin earrings in the shape of cornucopias, a sleeveless black satin blouse, tight pink slacks, and see-through plastic heels with rhinestone fish on them.

"Nice shoes," he commented. "Do you have a kid?" he inquired.

"Yeah, me." She laughed. "I started out collecting toys, then jewelry, and now I'm moving into memorabilia. Come on in the kitchen. I'm making hors d'oeuvres."

Zalman followed her down a hall lined with wood-block prints. "Who did these? They're great," he said.

"Rockwell Kent. Here we are."

The kitchen was straight out of a classy rendition of the Depression crossed with a definite tendency toward "Star Trek." There was a mammoth cream and green enamel stove against one wall, and another wall was covered with hanging kitchen utensils. The drainboards were pink and gray tile, the floor highly waxed spatter linoleum. A big refrigerator was plastered with magnetized replicas of monster-movie robots. A large plastic model of a spaceship—Zalman recognized it as the *Enterprise*—hung from the ceiling, and there was a complete set of dolls of the ship's crew in an old glass-fronted cabinet in the breakfast alcove.

"Is this a time warp?" He laughed.

"Collection," she said, working on a cunningly arranged shrimp plate. "Or maybe a time warp. Put the wine in the fridge."

Zalman opened the refrigerator, put the wine away, and helped himself to a little bottle of Perrier, then a shrimp off the plate Marie was arranging. "Snacks for me? I'm starved."

"Make yourself right at home," she said caustically.

"Thanks, Mom. I will. Mind if I look at the rest of the house? I love your decor. I'm a movie collector myself, film noir and gangster film stuff mainly."

"Really? I wouldn't peg you as a collector. Maybe Tiffany lamps or Oriental rugs, something upscale. Take a look around and if you see anything you like, I'll make you a good price," she said with a devilish smile.

"You ever read 'L'il Iodine' in the funnies? You remind me of her."

"I think I've been insulted," Marie camped. "Let me finish with this food. I thought we'd have a few hors d'oeuvres here, then go on to dinner."

Carrying his Perrier Zalman wandered back down the little hall and out into the living room, deciding Marie lived alone. Everything was too neat for two, and he felt unaccountably glad, though he wasn't sure why. She was too short for his taste and, besides, he liked blondes. He wandered down another hall into the bathroom, which was a shocking combination of pink and purple tiles with a vicious-looking swan etched in the frosted shower door. He peeked into a front bedroom, which was a sewing room-office fitted out with an old black and gold Singer, an ironing board, a golden oak desk topped with a regulation IBM electric, several glass-fronted bookcases containing what looked like collector's editions, and a lot of potted plants. He decided Marie definitely lived in the house rather than camped there between boyfriends and was unaccountably glad again.

"You own this place?" he called down the hall.

"Eight years," she called back.

"Smart girl." He retraced his steps through the toy store-living room, then went out a sliding glass door into a walled yard. Like the front of the house, flowers bloomed everywhere, and there was a tiny, picture-perfect vegetable garden plot in the middle of the little lawn, complete with a three-foot green plastic robot serving as scarecrow. There was even a small pond with a bubbling fountain, and Zalman walked over, looked into the blue water, and saw several large golden koi swimming lazily around a lily pad.

He went back inside and found her in the living room. The shrimp plate and long-stemmed glasses of wine were on Dagwood Bumstead's coffee table, and Zalman helped himself to another shrimp. "And she cooks, too?" he asked. "Marie, how come a nice, property-owning girl like yourself isn't married?"

"Never again," she said. "I've been married and I didn't like it."

"Come on," he goaded. "All girls want to get married."

"Many girls do. Some women do not. It didn't suit me and I don't do things I don't like."

"So what did you want to tell me that you didn't tell dear old dad?" he said suddenly.

"You trying to catch me off guard or something?" she asked suspiciously. "Finish your snacks and let's go. This place I'm taking you is very strict about reservations."

"You think your dad's got the place bugged? I wouldn't put it past the old weasel."

"He isn't that bad," she said defensively. "He's just . . . well . . ."

"A cop." Zalman laughed. "I've never met a guy who's more coppish. Okay, we'll go eat and you can tell me your tale of woe over dinner."

They took the Mercedes and Marie directed

him to a small private house in Pasadena, half an hour away by freeway. "Some friends of mine run this place," she explained. "It's very good. They only have six tables and they have to know you."

She was right, Zalman found. The three young women who cooked and served the dinner had impeccable taste. The food was beautifully cooked and presented, and the simple natural wood decor was quiet and tasteful. After he had finished his artichoke-stuffed chicken he leaned back in his chair, sipped his wine, and said, "Okay, doll. You've wined and dined me. Now spill."

She rolled her eyes. "What's with you and the snappy patter, Jerry? You sound like James M. Cain."

"I told you I collect noir. So level with me, sugar," he growled in a cross between Bogart and Garfield.

"All right." She laughed. "It isn't anything bad. Sticky Al used to ask me to hold things for him once in a while. He was a very secretive guy and he found out I have a little safe in the office and he'd ask me to keep his tickets from the track and pawn tickets and other little things and—"

"And you've got something of his now and that's what you don't want to tell Arnie? I don't blame you. What did Al give you lately?"

"I don't know," she said, twirling her wineglass. "It's in one of those padded envelopes. It's real little, whatever it is, 'cause the envelope's pretty small."

Zalman suddenly felt very happy. Maybe it was Hanning's ten thousand, and that would be one problem solved—a small problem, but it would make Phil happy. "It's at your office, I presume?"

"Nooooo," she said slowly. "After the . . . events of last night I decided to stash it somewhere else. You could open my little safe with a crowbar, and I guess I figured I owed it to Al to put the envelope away in a really safe place. Maybe his wife will want it or something. Anyway, it's at my place."

"Finish your dessert, angel," Zalman said. "Then you can pay the check and we'll go look at Sticky Al's envelope."

Marie was the first to see the disaster. When she opened the door to her little house her quick, sharp intake of breath told Zalman something was wrong. "Oh no!" she gasped. "Oh no . . ."

He elbowed her aside, stepped in, and saw that Dagwood Bumstead's living room looked like it had been hit by a hurricane. Furniture was upended, the sofa had been slashed, and many of the toys were knocked from their shelves.

"Get back in the car," Zalman ordered flatly. "Now!" he barked when she hesitated and opened her mouth to protest.

She turned and marched off, shoulders slumping with shock. Zalman turned on the lights and took a quick look around the house. Every room had been ripped apart, he noted, but only in a cursory fashion. Luckily, the damage was haphazard. A shelf of toys or dolls would be untouched next to a shelf that had been swept to the floor. Whoever wrecked the place, Zalman decided grimly, had been an amateur. But he was glad that at least Marie's little island of treasures hadn't been torched or completely destroyed.

He realized he was gripping the empty bottle of Pouilly-Fuissé he'd brought earlier like a club, and he put it down and went back out to the car. Marie sat staring forward stonily, her shoulders hunched with tension. "It's bad," he told her. "But not as bad as it looks."

She scowled at him like an auburn-maned bulldog. "This isn't just your casual robbery, right?" she said flatly. "It's about Sticky Al, isn't it?"

"And my jerk brother-in-law. Come on back in the house. I want to know what Sticky Al gave you to hold, assuming our friend the ransacker didn't get it."

"He didn't," she said with grim satisfaction, climbing out of the Mercedes. "I promise you."

They went back in the house and Zalman saw Marie try not to survey the wreckage as they made their way down the hall to the master bedroom. He had to admire her. For a girl with a trashed house she was awfully brave. When either of his ex-wives broke a fingernail they were Jell-O for weeks. All Marie said was "My dear little house . . ."

He followed her into the bedroom, which was the least damaged room in the place, and Zalman wondered fleetingly if the burglar had been intimidated by all the dolls. There were shelves and glass cases of teddy bears, stuffed toys of all types, china dolls, rag dolls, dolls with turn-of-the-century costumes, dolls with carved wooden heads and pioneer clothing, tin dolls, and plastic dolls. Curiously, they were mostly undisturbed.

The burglar had settled for ripping apart the bed and tossing Marie's clothes out of drawers onto the floor.

"You've got some collection," he said. "I'm impressed."

She nodded dully, picking up a handful of clothes and laying them over a chair, then sat down and rummaged around in a pile of dolls that were tossed on the bed. "Here it is," she said triumphantly. "I knew nobody could find it." She held up a large celluloid doll dressed in an elaborate yellow satin flapper's outfit. Carefully, she unscrewed its head and reached into the body cavity. "I've had Minky here since I was a kid. Always used to hide my secret stuff in here." She gently eased a small padded mailing envelope from the doll's body and handed it to Zalman.

Zalman opened it and a metal pin about three inches in diameter fell into his hand. The pin was white enamel on the front and brass on the back. It was the sort of item that had been practically a giveaway in the midsixties, judging from the legend on the front where jaunty red and blue letters proclaimed I'M A BEATLES FAN. IN CASE OF EMERGENCY CALL PAUL!

"What the hell!" Zalman exploded. "This is what Sticky Al gave you to hold for him?"

Marie took the pin and, tired as she was, looked it over with a professional eye. "I didn't know Al was into collecting," she said with a little laugh. "Beatles stuff is skyrocketing, you know. Al was always trying to promote a quick buck and maybe he decided to get in on the craze."

"Jesus." Zalman sighed. He'd been hoping to find Hanning's ten thousand dollars. And besides, the idea that Sticky Al Hix might have been killed for a crummy Beatles pin was too depressing. Zalman put the pin in his pocket and realized he was very tired. "Listen, angel," he said, "how about you come and camp at my place."

She turned dark eyes on him in mock amazement. "Isn't this kind of sudden? What about the soft lights, the dancing and romancing? I figured an uptown guy like you would lead me on, ply me with fine wines . . ."

"My intentions are strictly honorable, at this point anyway. The goon who so kindly tidied up your house might just decide to come back. So, unless you want to call your pop . . . ?"

"No way, José," she said. "A crime-prevention lecture isn't what I need at this point. Just a second while I throw some stuff in a bag."

Minutes later they drove away from the quiet street of quiet houses and were quiet themselves as Zalman drove to his own house in the hills. Marie hunched down in the passenger's seat, hands buried in the pockets of her batwing satin jacket, her face a blank mask. Twenty minutes later they arrived at his street-level garage, and she followed him down the seastone walkway to his front door and stood quietly while he unlocked it, stepped inside, and flipped on the lights.

"Goddamn!" he exploded. "Son of a bitch to hell!" His house had been trashed just as Marie's house had been trashed. "Get in the car," he told her wearily. This time she turned and trudged away without protest.

He went in, turning on lights, surveying the wreckage from room to room. It was obvious the same person who'd ransacked Marie's house was responsible for destroying his place. There was the same haphazard pattern of destruction. In the living room the big couch had been slashed, but the armchair next to it had been ignored. A bookcase had been turned over and volumes scattered on the floor, but a second bookcase across the room hadn't been touched. Silver had been tossed out of a sideboard in the dining room, but from what Zalman could see none of the pieces were missing. He went into his bedroom. As with Marie's bedroom, clothing had been thrown from bureau drawers onto the floor and some of his suits had been torn from hangers and flung about. But overall, he concluded grimly, the damage wasn't too bad. At least his movie posters were intact.

"I'm going to get you, you son of a bitch," he said aloud, "wherever you are. No kidding." Quickly he packed a few clothes and toiletries in a Gucci overnight bag, punched the call-forward function on his phone, left the lights burning, locked the door, and returned to Marie in the Mercedes.

"Where to now, Jerry?" she asked as he tossed the bag in the back seat.

"There's one place in L.A. that's safe from everything up to and probably including a frontal tank attack," he told her as he gunned the car down the hill. "The Compound."

"Sounds like a military school," she quipped weakly.

"It's Doyle Dean McCoy's joint up in Newhall," he explained, wheeling onto the Hollywood northbound. "You haven't met my old chum McCoy but take it from me, we'll be safe there."

"Jerry," she asked after a minute. "Who's doing this to us? I mean, what've we done that's so bad?"

"It's a long story, toots, and I don't understand it myself. Suffice it to say we've stepped into the middle of something and even though we don't mean to we're making somebody very nervous. By the way, our pal the intruder is a good hand with a lockpick. I don't know if you noticed but the locks weren't forced at either house and windows weren't broken. That means our friend let himself in."

"Oh boy," Marie said with a tight smile. "Daddy's going to love this. He's always lecturing me about how I should get some security around my house. You know, bars on the windows, triple locks, electronic wailers, a dog."

Thirty minutes later Zalman pulled the Mercedes up to a high cyclone-fence gate at the end of a long, winding dirt road in the hills east of Newhall. A sign on the gate read "Private. This means you!" Underneath it a second sign read "Protected by Smith & Wesson," while a third sign read "Make my day!" Zalman leaned out, pushed a speaker button, and a moment later McCoy's voice barked, "State your business!"

"It's Zalman. Let me in."

McCoy laughed maniacally. "Zalman? How do I know it's Zalman? How many bones has the carpus?"

"Oh Jesus," Zalman muttered. "Cut it out, McCoy," he yelled into the speaker. "I'm in no mood for tricks."

McCoy laughed again. "Too bad for you then. No tickee no laundry."

"What's going on?" Marie asked.

"Quiet, quiet. I'll get you for this, McCoy!" Zalman cudgeled his brain. "Eight bones has the goddamn carpus! Now open the goddamn gate!"

"And . . ." McCoy prompted.

Zalman ground his teeth. "'Eight bones has the carpus,'" he singsonged, trying to keep the ditty straight in his mind. "'Five the metacarpus. Fourteen the phalanges. All in all, all in all, twenty-seven, all in all.' Okay? Satisfied it's me? Now open the goddamn gate!"

The speakerphone hissed static and the electric gate moved smoothly back on its oiled track. Zalman swore under his breath and gunned the car up the driveway.

"What was that all about?" Marie inquired as they followed the narrow, winding road through a grove of eucalyptus.

"A few years back I made a big mistake and got my friend McCoy interested in old movies. That business about the carpus is his password. It's a little thing from *The Beast with Five Fingers*. The movie about the crazed hand?"

"With Michael Caine?"

"No, the original, with Alan Alda's dad. Never mind. It's not important now."

They cleared the trees and saw McCoy waiting for them out in front of a long green mobile home on top of a small hill. He was surrounded by yapping Dobermans, waving his flashlight at the trees, and the dogs were having a great time trying to chase the light. "Sic 'em, Millard!" McCoy laughed. "Get 'em, Grover!" The dogs ran back and forth in a frenzy of joyful excitement.

Zalman pulled the Mercedes to a stop with a

flurry of crunching gravel. "Thanks a lot, McCoy," he said. "Just what I need, trying to remember how many bones has the goddamn carpus!"

"Had to be sure it was you, Jerry," McCoy said, grinning. "Who's your pretty friend?"

"Doyle Dean McCoy," Zalman said, "may I present Marie Thrasher?" Zalman hoisted the overnight bags out of the car while Marie marched up to McCoy and shook hands.

"Pleased to meetcha," McCoy mumbled. "Goddamn it, Calvin," he barked at a dog, "don't chew on Chester!" McCoy smiled apologetically at Marie. "Company gets 'em crazy," he explained.

McCoy led the way inside, past a humming washer and dryer in the entryway, into the big, cluttered living room of his double-wide. Rutherford, the Doberman in disgrace, sprawled moodily on a huge Western-style sofa, poking his moist snout through one of the wagon-wheel arms. As soon as he saw Marie he perked up, slunk over, and sniffed her. "What a nice boy!" Marie cooed, bending down and gently fondling Rutherford's pointed little ears. He gave her a doggy grin and rubbed against her ingratiatingly.

"I'll be damned," McCoy muttered. "That meatsack hasn't gotten up for anything 'cept eats since he was a pup. You must be a dog person, Marie. He sure likes you."

"All animals are okay with me," she said, still ruffling the dog's ears. "Except snakes. I have a thing about snakes."

"They're ugly-looking things all right," McCoy agreed. "Every summer I get a few rattlers around here. Have to blow 'em away. So what's up, Jerry?"

"Give us a drink and I'll fill you in," Zalman said with a tired wave, trying not to dwell on McCoy's decor, which consisted of Western-motif furniture, gun racks full of weaponry, and gray metal shelving containing hundreds of video cassette copies of old movies. While McCoy rustled up some drugstore brand whiskey and ice, Zalman told him the events of the evening. "So I thought Marie and I would camp here tonight," he concluded.

"Damned right." McCoy grinned evilly, taking a long pull on one of his ever-present bottles of beer. "You want protection, you come to McCoy. No problem. Like I told Marie there, I see any snakes around here I just blow 'em away."

"You find out anything about Mrs. Al?" Zalman asked.

McCoy shook his head. "She ain't around, Jerry. The joint up in Thousand Jokes you gave me the address for? She ain't there. Neighbor lady says Mrs. Al and the kid took off a few nights ago and nobody knows where the hell they went. I got it organized though. This lady's going to give me a ring if they come back."

"How much is all this costing?" Zalman asked suspiciously.

"Shucks, Jerry," McCoy said bashfully. "A couple hours of my time is all. Don't worry, she'll phone. Hey," he called to Marie, "Is he bothering you?" Rutherford was now lying at Marie's feet, lapping gently at her ankle with his long pink tongue.

"No." Marie laughed, trying not to spill her

drink. "He's just darling. I thought Dobermans were supposed to be mean." She leaned down and scratched the dog's head, and he turned over and exposed his belly. "What a good woojums," Marie murmured as Rutherford greased his snout on her leg.

Zalman looked at McCoy and shook his head. "Looks like another first for Rutherford. Hey, you can put us up, right?"

"Sure," McCoy said, lighting a Lucky. "I got a spare room, just like uptown."

"I'll sleep on the couch tonight," Zalman interjected quickly before McCoy made any further comments about the sleeping arrangements. "Tomorrow maybe I'll go to a hotel or something. We'll see."

"Sure you will." McCoy grinned, giving Zalman a vaudeville wink. Zalman glanced over at Marie to see if she'd noticed, but she was too busy talking baby talk to Rutherford.

"Cootsie wootsie *likes* to have his chin scratched," she crooned. "What a *sweet* boy it is, sweeeeeet boy." Rutherford began to emit tiny little chuffs of happiness.

Zalman and McCoy looked at each other in horror. Rutherford rolled his eyes at Marie. "Ever see Eddie Cantor in *Whoopee?*" McCoy asked slowly. "Dog looks just like him."

"I think I've got to get some sleep," Marie announced. McCoy led her down the hall, showed her the spare room and the bathroom, and then came back into the living room. They heard Marie clatter about in the bathroom for a few minutes and then shut the door to the bedroom. Rutherford immediately began to howl at the door until she let him in.

"Looks like true love," Zalman said.

"Jerry, are you out of your mind or what? That little lamikins is Arnie Thrasher's daughter!"

"Not me, you idiot! Her and Rutherford! She's too short for me."

"Right. Sure," McCoy said. "You must be about a quart low if you think I believe that. On the other hand, you're too old for these six-foot blondes. You ought to get involved with a girl who's as smart as you are."

"What the hell are you talking about?" Zalman exploded. "You think you're Dr. Ruth?"

"Shut up, she'll hear us. One bad thing about mobile homes is you can hear everything through the walls."

"McCoy," Zalman said, making a serious effort to regain his composure, "Miss Marie Thrasher is a very nice young lady. She's very attractive if you like short redheads, which I do not. Besides, I *know* she's Arnie Thrasher's daughter. Believe me, Arnie made sure to mention it to me. This thing is all a mistake. It's all Phil's fault, that lying cretin. Look, I didn't even know she was Arnie's daughter until after we found the body. Anyway," he concluded, "*she* opened the refrigerator. I was just standing around—"

"Looking at her chest, I'll bet."

"Well, she's short, but hell, I'm only human."

"First sign I've seen of it."

Zalman buried his head in his hands. "I'm losing my mind. This is how it starts. Everything begins to look like it's right out of German Expressionism, sort of like prewar Berlin."

"Kinda *Cabinet of Dr. Caligari*? I know what you mean," McCoy said, stretching out his long legs on a footstool that looked like a saddle. "I'm just telling you, Jerry, Arnie's going to have your bones for barbecue if you mess with his daughter. Couldn't you get involved with somebody safe, like a Mafia princess, maybe?"

"That's it, I'm going to sleep. I can't take any more of this."

McCoy began to laugh. "That's what you think, pal o' mine."

They turned in and Zalman drifted uncomfortably off to sleep on the wagon-wheel couch, which stank of dogs, cigarette smoke, and TV dinners. But he didn't sleep long.

At four that morning he was awakened by the sound of a ringing phone. He sat up straight and reached for the infernal thing, but of course it wasn't next to his bed because he wasn't in his bed. He was on McCoy's couch, his hand connected with thinnest air, and the phone went on bleating. He forced himself up off the couch and fumbled into the kitchen, bumping his shin against a table leg as he groped around in the dark. "Yes?" he said unpleasantly as he grabbed the phone.

"Zally?" Phil Hanning's voice asked. Zalman said nothing. "Zally," Hanning repeated. "Somebody stole the DeLorean." Zalman groaned.

An hour and a half later, bleary but nonetheless shaved and dressed, Zalman pulled up in front of the Hannings' immense neo-Colonial manse abutting the Toluca Lake golf course and noted the house was ablaze with lights. As he made his way to the front door he could hear his sister's rage troubling the chill predawn air.

"My car!" she was shrieking, and judging by her raw tone of voice he figured she'd been screaming for some time. "I love that car, Phil!"

71

she shrieked as Zalman let himself in. "Why, Phil? Why?"

"Calm down, for the love of Mike." Zalman winced, stepping down into the huge sunken living room where Lucille, clad in a fluffy white terrycloth robe, was stalking back and forth on the fluffy white carpeting. "Phil, get me some coffee," he shouted, then sat down on one of the dead white linen chairs which matched the dead white linen couch, the dead white walls, and the ten by twelve dead white painting Bland had done while in the throes of an acid trip in the late seventies. Zalman hated the room. It always gave him a headache.

"I swear I'm gonna kill the bastard!" Lucille growled between puffs of a Benson & Hedges. "He hocked my car, can you believe it? Then he didn't pay off and naturally somebody came and took the car." Without warning she picked up a crystal ashtray the size of a small cantaloupe and pitched it through the big sliding glass window out onto the deck. The shattering glass made a terrific racket, and then all was silence except for the quiet lapping of wind-ruffled pool water beyond the gaping hole.

Zalman applauded. "Feel better, dear?" he asked his sister unpleasantly. "Hanning!" he barked. "Get me some goddamned coffee and make a note to phone the glass company." A terrified Phil Hanning, clad in a thick white terrycloth robe, poked his head around the swinging louvered doors to the kitchen, sized up the broken window, and retreated.

Abruptly, Lucille sat down, coughed smoke, and stared grimly at her brother. "He hocked my DeLorean for ten thousand measly bucks," she said in measured tones. "All for this stupid auction thing. I believe I will either kill him or divorce him."

"Better reverse the order then," Zalman advised. "Lucille, my dear, please go to bed now and watch 'Good Morning America' or something equally educational and leave me to discuss matters with your husband."

Lucille glared at the saloon doors concealing Hanning, glared at the broken window, and glared at Zalman. "I don't like this," she said flatly. She left without another word.

"Come on out, Phil," Zalman called. "She's gone to get videoed. The coast is clear."

Hanning crept cautiously into the living room, carrying a mug of coffee for Zalman and a bottle of Black Label for himself. "Zally," he moaned, "this time Lucille's *really* gonna slaughter me."

"I don't blame her," Zalman said, slugging down his coffee. "It had to be the DeLorean? You know what that car means to her. Look, you gotta level with me. Who gave you the money for the car?"

Hanning drank straight from the bottle. He stared apprehensively at the broken window. "You know that guy you introduced me to that time we had lunch at Le Croque, the guy on TV? The car dealer who wears all those funny costumes all the time? You know who I mean?"

Zalman did indeed know whom he meant. "Not 'Matchstick Slim Sells New Cars Jim?'" he asked in horror, quoting "Matchstick Slim" Honniger's well-known TV commercial. "You went to Matchstick Slim for money? Phil, you should be committed. You're certifiable, you know that? You're . . ." he groped for words, "criminally stupid!"

"Zally, come on . . ."

"Come on nothing, pal. You borrow ten thou on the DeLorean, which is easily worth fifty K. You lie to me about where you got the money. You don't pay it back on time. What did you think Slim was going to do?"

"Zally, I thought he'd give me a little more time. This deal is just taking a little longer than I planned, what with Al dead and all and the money supposedly missing. Under the circumstances I thought—"

"You thought!" Zalman exploded. "Please allow me to tell you something, pal. In your entire life, even before, a thought is something you've never experienced!" Sobered by his unrehearsed outburst Zalman wrenched the bottle out of Hanning's grip, sloshed a liberal dollop of scotch into his empty coffee mug, and drank deeply. "Okay, Phil," he said at last, struggling to regain composure. "I'm sorry I shouted, but all I can say is words fail me. Lucille!"

"Yah, mein Kapitan!" Lucille said, reappearing in the doorway. She saluted germanically. "I await your orders."

"I think I've got the picture here," Zalman told her. "Phil's involved with Slim Honniger, who's a client of mine—"

"Oh Christ," Lucille moaned. "Matchstick Slim has my car?"

"Pipe down. I'll work something out," Zalman told his sister.

"I'll pay the ten thousand," Lucille affirmed. "No problem. All I want is my goddamn car back in one piece."

"You may have to pay more than ten thou, thanks to Mr. Financial Genius here," Zalman said. "But we'll attend to that later. Meanwhile, Lucille, listen to me carefully. You must keep

Phil under house arrest. Don't let him go out, okay?"

"I got a big meeting today at CBS," Lucille whined.

"You work it out somehow," Zalman ordered, shooting her a stern look. "He's weak. He's spineless. He's got no character."

"It's true," Hanning said moodily, slugging from the bottle. "It's all true."

"Put a leash on him if you have to," Zalman suggested. All he wanted now was to get out of the zoo and breathe some fresh air. "Talk to me later," he called, stepping out the front door into a purple-pink dawn breaking over the Tujunga foothills, bathing the Valley in soft hues. As he climbed back in his trusty Mercedes he wondered what new madness the fresh day would bring in its wake.

After he escaped the Hannings Zalman went home to his ruined house and tried to straighten up a little, had a long soak in the tub, and put in a call to Isobel, his cleaning and maintenance expert, without success. He left word with her service and she called him back as he was getting dressed.

"Isobel! I'm glad you called. Look, dear, I've got a major cleaning problem which demands your attention. How soon can you get here?"

There was a long pause. Isobel saw herself as a professional; she had a very tight schedule and brooked no interference from her clients, who were so grateful to find someone who didn't steal, made a vague effort to clean their houses, and showed up more or less regularly that they were willing to put up with her sharp tongue. "Today? You've got to be kidding, Jerry. But look, I'm glad you called. I've been wanting to talk to you about Undie World. You *have* heard of Undie World?" she asked in a tone which suggested that anyone who hadn't heard of Undie World simply wasn't a vertebrate.

"Sure I have," he said, wondering what kind of fool scheme Isobel was involved with this time. He'd known her for five years, and in that time Isobel had gone through various pyramids, Amway, Tupperware, Herbalife, and a gold-from-seawater scheme that would have made a fourteenth-century alchemist blush. "Look, Isobel, I need help here."

"What did you do," she asked suspiciously, "have another one of those parties of yours? See, Undie World is a terrific sales opportunity for the truly motivated person. I invite my friends over and feed them drinks and we have models who show them all this nasty lingerie. Stuff they'd be embarrassed to even *look* at in a store . . . I spoke to you about your parties, Jerry. I do cleaning work, and I like to think of myself as a professional, but you know and I know I'm only doing this until I can unleash my entrepreneurial talents. Undie World *could* be the big one."

"It sounds good, Isobel, it really does," Zalman soothed. "But look, I've got an emergency and only you can help me out on this. It wasn't a party, I swear it. It was worse. I was . . . robbed," he said quickly. What the hell. It was almost true.

"Robbed! Robbed! I thought you had a security system! I don't like working for people who don't have topflight security! Didn't you see *Death Wish II*? Do you know the kind of thing that can happen while you're cleaning a house? Honestly, Jerry, you're really too much . . ." She trailed off.

"Isobel, look, I promise I'll have a security system put in if you'll just help me out on this. There'll be a bonus in it for you," he said, hoping the lure of extra cash might bring out the brigand in her.

"That's not the point, Jerry," she said sharply. "Financial arrangements aren't the issue here. All right, I'll come over. It'll mean making other people very unhappy, but I'll see what I can do. Look, I'll leave the Undie World brochure for you. I'd like to get your thoughts on this."

"Okay, Isobel," Zalman capitulated. "I appreciate the extra effort. Do the best you can with it, okay? I know it's bad, but just do what you can."

"I always do, Jerry," she huffed as she hung up the phone.

Zalman was relieved. Making a deal with Isobel was tougher than a negotiation with the Internal Revenue Service. He called his secretary, Esther Wong, to find out what calls she'd received that morning and had a lot of fun trying to guess the names of various clients which Esther had forgotten. He drank some orange juice and ate a soft-boiled egg and, these tasks accomplished, a refreshed Jerry Zalman turned once more to matters at hand.

It was ten-thirty. The morning was pleasant and the freeways leading out to the San Fernando Valley were little more than three-quarters full with motorists playing the adult version of bumper cars. Zalman tried to listen to Bland's latest tape on the drive but found Bland's particular brand of heavy metal nauseating. He even tried to sing along but to no avail. It was hard to join in on a song that consisted of a very limited melody and an endlessly repeated lyric: "inna coma inna coma inna coma . . ."

Forty minutes later he glided the Mercedes to a gentle stop in front of a car lot in Van Nuys that easily covered ten acres. There was a two-story sign in Day-Glo pink bearing the legend "Matchstick Slim Sells New Cars Jim" and a second large sign featuring the painted image of Matchstick Slim Honniger dressed as a jolly clown, his favorite trademark. Overhead, anchored by guy wires, a gigantic hot-air clown balloon drifted in the smog-laden air, grinning with malevolent glee.

"Jesus," Zalman muttered as he looked around, blinded by the sharp morning light glinting off several hundred washed chrome grills and highly waxed car hoods.

A young salesman with a handlebar mustache and different-colored eyes bore down on him like a shark through the sea of cars. Zalman held up an admonishing hand and fixed the youngster with a stern glare. "I'm not here to buy a car. I'm looking for Mr. Honniger. Know where he is?"

The salesman circled him relentlessly, looking for an opening. "I've got a great Porsche Speedster," he said. "Red, '58. You'd look great in it. It's got your name on it, Mr. . . ."

"I like the Mercedes," Zalman said dryly. "I'm looking for Mr. Honniger."

The young salesman with the mismatched eyes realized Zalman was in fact looking for Mr. Honniger and not a used Porsche. He shrugged and pointed toward the back of the lot. "They're out there," he said indifferently, "shooting." Before Zalman could find out exactly where in back they were shooting, the salesman sprinted away toward a young couple staring greedily at a chromed-up van.

Zalman sighed, then trudged through what seemed like miles of cars and finally found Matchstick Slim Honniger shooting a commercial at that very moment. True to his nickname, Slim was indeed slim. He was also well over six feet, weighed in at one-eighty or so, and wore a lounge lizard mustache that, combined with his billiard ball head, made him look like Mr. Clean in drag as Zachary Scott.

Today, Matchstick Slim was dressed as the same fat clown whose evil image floated over the entrance to his car emporium. Costumes were Slim's trademark, and in each commercial he wore an elaborate, fancy getup. The clown was his favorite, but he'd gone punk, had done a giant chicken, a hobo, a cowboy, Dracula, a knight in full armor, and anything else he could think of to persuade some sucker to make an easy down payment on a heap from "Matchstick Slim Sells New Cars Jim," although in point of fact Slim pushed "pre-used" vehicles as well. In the neo-jungle world of L.A. car dealerships, Slim believed a mind-boggling gimmick was what it took, and judging from the size and evident prosperity of the business his judgment was right on the money.

Slim didn't twitch a whisker when he caught sight of Zalman standing on the sidelines next to a beefy kid balancing a big portable video pack on his shoulders. He merely inclined his bald head and continued his nutty clown spiel. But when the take was over Slim strode to Zalman's side, peeled off his giant white rubber gloves, and shook hands. The clown outfit was easily five feet wide at the middle, and since Slim was more than a foot taller than Zalman they made a regular Mutt and Jeff pair.

"So, Jerry . . ." Slim beamed down. "Time for a new car or what?"

"Or what, Slimbo." Zalman smiled pleasantly. "Let's talk in your office if you're through out there."

"Boy, I'll tell you I'm through." Slim gasped, pulling at his neck ruff. "This goddamn suit is hotter than—"

"An Arizona dune buggy?" Zalman suggested, grinning.

Slim blanched beneath his jovial makeup. "Keep it down, willya?" he said nervously. "You're a great legal beagle, Jerry, which is why I come to you when I got trouble, but you got a sharp mouth, you know that?"

Zalman simply smiled, enjoying his little joke. He happened to know that although Slim Honniger had been in the car business most of his adult life he hadn't always sold cars. First he'd stolen them, and later on when things got too messy he'd gone legit and opened a lot. "It's easier to be legal," he'd told Zalman years before when they first became associated, and nowadays very few people other than Jerry Zalman remembered Slim's murky beginnings.

Half an hour later Zalman and Slim were in his mammoth brown Formica office enjoying the air conditioning. Slim looked much more comfortable in a livid green polyester leisure suit with pink saddle-stitching, and aside from some flecks of white pancake makeup still embedded in his mustache there was nothing to suggest that he'd ever been a roly-poly clown.

"Those cars are pretty all lined up like that," Slim mused lyrically, staring through his big upstairs window as they waited for his secretary to bring a couple of tumblers of iced tea. "Terrible what some jerks do to a car. I mean, they're delicate machines. I send the poor things out of here all shined up, tuned up, ready to go, and six months later they're back looking like hell. It's a crime." The iced tea arrived and Slim sipped, put his glass on his desk, picked up a blue yachting cap, and cocked it at a rakish angle on his shiny dome.

Zalman, sipping his own tea, couldn't help noticing a large metal pin nestled next to the cap's gold braid emblem. The pin was about three inches in diameter and bore the legend I'M A BEATLES FAN. IN CASE OF EMERGENCY CALL RINGO. Zalman looked at the pin with a dawning sense of recognition, gears clicking into place in his brain. "Speaking of crime," he said brightly, "you seen my sister's DeLorean by any chance?"

Slim looked at the toes of his cowboy boots, then the surface of his desk, then made a minute study of his tumbler of iced tea. "Listen, Zally," he said apprehensively, "that was strictly business, nothing personal against you or Phil. I mean, the guy comes to me to borrow some dough. It sounded okay at the time, especially with the DeLorean as collateral, but after Al gets killed I hear Henderson never got the front money. Okay, I'm willing to eat the ten I kicked in personally, but not the ten I loaned Phil. I had to tell the boys to go get the car. I didn't steal it, y'know. I repossessed it. I got the pink slip and everything."

"Jesus," Zalman moaned. "Say it ain't so. Twenty thou?"

"Hey, help me out, willya?" Slim protested. "Phil says him and Sticky Al Hix have a line on this Henderson thing and he needs ten thou to buy in. Al's part is the connection so he don't need any dough 'cause he's setting up the deal. Phil offers the car as security and I figure what the hey. I even take a flyer on it myself just for fun. I give him the cash and he gives me this button, sort of like a marker. He has one, Al has one . . ."

Zalman reached into his pocket and pulled out the CALL PAUL button. "Sticky Al had one," he corrected. "Now Jerry Zalman has one. Come on, Slim, how many guys were in on this deal? You, Phil, Sticky Al . . . ?"

"Far as I know it's just us and the guy on the radio all the time—you know who I mean. See, this is supposed to be the world's biggest collection of rock-and-roll stuff: pins, buttons, dolls, lunch boxes, pencils, scarves, posters, records, everything." Slim shrugged. "Sounds like junk, right? But I checked around and people tell me this stuff is gold, brings real money, Jerry. So the part about Count Monty sounds good to me since I figure he'd know if the stuff is genuine."

"Count Monty, the DJ?" Zalman asked, although he knew full well that in the whole of the greater Los Angeles Basin there was only one Count Monty. For close to fifteen years Count Monty had literally owned the late night airwaves, his gravelly voice throbbing out across the freeways, creating an instant brotherhood of hard-core audio maniacs. The sheer volume of his rock and roll consoled on even the darkest nights, while the dynamic force of his charismatic persona convinced fans he was ten feet tall and able to leap tall buildings. Count Monty was a fourteen-karat living legend.

"That's right," Slim affirmed. "Look, Zally, Phil's a sweetheart but, you'll pardon the reference, he's five bricks short of a load. And Sticky Al I've known for years and wouldn't turn my back on him for love or money. But Count Monty's a legit guy, so that's why I went ahead and took a flyer on this thing. I mean, what do I know about rock and roll? I'm just a car dealer."

"You're a car thief is what you are," Zalman said pleasantly. "So where's the DeLorean?"

"I got it out back. Tell you the truth, Jerry," Slim said shrewdly, "I wasn't all that surprised to see you this morning. I didn't plan on doing anything with the car right away anyhow since I figured you'd want to work something out."

"The hell with that," Zalman said. "Let my sister stick hot knives in Phil's gut for a few days. He needs it. Now I have a few words of professional wisdom for you, my friend. Be careful, be cautious. This antique deal has turned sour, in case you haven't caught on. First, somebody put a hole in Sticky Al and loaded him in the fridge. By the way, you know anything about that?"

"Jeez, Zally," Slim protested with a great show of sincerity, diamond pinky rings glinting in the fluorescent light. "I didn't dislike Al that much. And besides, why would I go stealing my own money, for Christ's sake? I got the DeLorean to show for my twenty grand so I'm already ahead."

"Right," Zalman said dryly, resuming his finger ticking. "Second, I find the body, which I do not like. And third, last night my house is trashed and so is a lady friend of mine's, and I have a strong feeling it's all because of these little buttons here," he said, tapping his CALL PAUL button.

"I'm a very careful guy, Jerry," Slim said smoothly. "That's how come I got to be so old. Don't worry about me."

Zalman drained his tea and stood up. "Don't sell the car, Slimbo. Phil will make good on it."

Slim raised his eyebrows. "You guarantee it?"

"Don't worry about it," Zalman said heartily. "Trust me. In fact, as your lawyer I'm advising you not to do anything. Put the button away, and if you hear from Count Monty or Phil or if Sticky Al speaks to you from beyond the grave, call me. Talk to me later," he called, heading for the door.

Outside Slim Honniger's office the day was heating up, and after hiking back through the sea of cars Zalman was glad to reach the air-conditioned privacy of the Mercedes. He pulled onto the San Diego Freeway, picked up the car phone, and dialed McCoy's number. Marie Thrasher answered, sounding very subdued.

"So, shorty," Zalman said, "you want to have lunch? I'm hungry and besides I want to ask you some penetrating questions, as the girl said to the sailor."

She was silent for a couple of beats. "Penetrating, huh? What's all that noise? Where are you?"

"On the freeway. Where's McCoy?"

"He went to look for Mrs. Al. I just got out of the shower. Jerry, you're not gonna like this. I called my office a little while ago and guess what Linda told me? Somebody ransacked Type-it last night. Tore the place up and smashed open my safe."

"I guess we should have figured," Zalman

said a second later after he'd digested this latest dispatch. "Somebody hits both our houses. It makes sense he'll get your office. Not my office though. We've got heavy electronic security in my building. Get dressed," he said suddenly, because he figured she needed to be jollied and also because the image of her in the shower was making him itchy. "I'll pick you up in half an hour, we'll go eat, and you'll feel better. Listen for me at the gate. The password is 'carpus.'" He heard her giggle in spite of herself; then he hung up and took a lungful of filtered, lead-laden air. "I mean it," he muttered. "Whoever you are, I'm gonna get you, you bastard."

She was ready to go when he got to McCoy's, dressed in jeans and a denim work shirt knotted fetchingly at the waist, sleeves rolled up, and cleavage attractively evident. "I didn't bring much with me," she said, "so I appropriated one of McCoy's shirts." Rutherford was at her side and whined piteously when she got into the car. "Come on, Jerry," she wheedled, "can Ruthie-poo go with us?"

"Jesus," Zalman muttered. "I feel like Roy Earle and Pard. Okay, tell him to get in back and don't let him rip the upholstery." Rutherford piled in back with a slobbery doggy grin and they were off down the dirt road.

"Who's Roy Earle and Pard?" Marie asked listlessly. Clearly, the break-in at Typeit was one ransacking too many and she was on the verge of depression.

"The character Bogart played in *High Sierra* and Pard was Ida Lupino's dog, but that's not important right now. Where do you want to eat?"

"I don't care as long as it's good," she said

morosely, stroking Rutherford's head, which was draped over the back of the seat. "Where were you all morning?"

"Sleuthing. Marie, I'm sorry about your office," he told her, noticing that the blue shirt looked a lot different on her than it did on McCoy.

"At least no one was there when it happened so no one got hurt, thank God," Marie said, staring out the window. "I told Linda not to bother calling the cops. I'd just have to explain about Sticky Al and the houses last night and everything and then Daddy'd find out and I decided better to let it ride." She shrugged.

"Want to play detective today?" Zalman asked briskly, patting her arm. "I want to find out some more about this auction."

"Okay," she agreed, brightening a little. "I flipped when I saw that Beatles pin. Can I have it when you're through with it? God, I could just kill myself for not picking up more Beatles stuff when they were hot."

Zalman told her what Matchstick Slim had told him about the auction. "Tell me seriously, in your professional opinion as a collector," he asked, guiding the car back onto the freeway, "do you think this rock-and-roll stuff is worth anything?"

"Depends on what they have to sell. Beatles stuff, yeah, sure. Elvis stuff, you can clean up with it. Of course, if I had a lot of Beatles stuff I'd hold onto it for ten years if I could. The stuff can only appreciate. Failing nuclear war, in ten years that pin'll easily be worth a hundred bucks, maybe more."

A little while later Zalman pulled into the

small parking lot behind Moe Zelnick's hot dog stand in West L.A., jumped out of the car, and opened the door for Marie. The stand was tiny and, besides serving the best hot dogs in town, it had the added attraction of being shaped like a giant hot dog, complete with mustard dripping off the edges of the roll. "You like chili dogs?" he asked, holding the car door for her. "I got a yen for a chili dog."

Marie managed a laugh as she and Rutherford got out. "I underestimated you, Mr. Attorney. I thought you were a culinary snob and here I find you're really a man of the people. Yeah, I gotta yen . . ."

Zalman suddenly took her in his arms and kissed her with all the aplomb and expertise he could muster. He heard a burst of applause from the patrons sitting at the counter, and when he thought he'd kissed her sufficiently he stood away, turned to them, made a mock heel-clicking bow, and offered her his arm. "Now," he inquired blandly, "you ready for that chili dog?"

She laughed again, more heartily this time, and pressed her body into his. "Mr. Attorney," she said, "I believe I'm ready for anything."

Marie and Zalman ate a pair of chili dogs each and washed them down with Moe Zelnick's specially made egg creams, while Rutherford had a plain dog on a bun and a paper bowl of water which Zelnick thoughtfully provided. "For Zally, anything." Zelnick beamed over his relish-stained bib apron. To Zalman he whispered heavily, "A nice girl. Good-looking and a healthy appetite. Could you ask for more?"

"So what do we do now?" Marie asked as she

wiped the last of the mustard from her lips. The food had done her good and she'd picked up a little.

"An interesting question, Watson," Zalman said thoughtfully. "You wait here. I'll make a couple calls." As he walked to his car he heard her discussing egg cream recipes with Zelnick.

Zalman slid into the Mercedes and called his office. Esther reeled off a list of people who'd phoned since morning, and he gave her a terse set of instructions as to whom to call back and whom to ignore. This out of the way, he told her to phone Lucille's office.

"Get hold of that kid who works for her," Zalman said, "Dex, and tell him to find out Count Monty's address and number. Then phone Monty, explain who I am and that I want to see him. If he makes any trouble tell him it's on Lucille's behalf. Sometime this afternoon would be great. I'm at Zelnick's so take my driving time into account when you make the appointment. Call me back soonest." He hung up and went back to the counter.

". . . so whaddya think, my wife's a chemist?" Zelnick said, his bald head bobbing merrily as he delivered his punch line with an air of triumph. He and Marie broke into laughter.

"Now what?" Marie asked Zalman, still giggling.

"Now we drink coffee, admire the traffic, and wait," he told her.

The car phone rang barely five minutes later and Esther responded with Count Monty's entire résumé, courtesy of Dex. "And Count Monty said he could really get behind talking to you," Esther gushed, "because he's got a few legal problems himself and has heard you're the greatest."

"Good work, Esther," Zalman said as he jotted down Count Monty's address. "If I make any money off this guy I'll send you to La Costa for your vacation—deal?"

"Oooooo, nifty!" she squealed. "Bye . . ."

"Come on, shorty," he called to Marie, waving to Zelnick at the same time. "We're off to see the wizard."

COUNT MONTY HAD BEEN AROUND THE L.A. music world nearly fifteen years, and for a guy who wasn't yet forty that was going some. He lived in a rambling Spanish mansion on top of Laurel Canyon which, according to Dex in Lucille's office, he'd bought for an absurdly low sum when both rock and roll and real estate were young. Now he was sitting on a multi-million-dollar hunk of property.

Zalman wheeled the Mercedes into the circular driveway, noting the expensive cars strewn around like Hot Wheels. "Okay, shorty," he told Marie before they got out. "Act dim—got it?" He saw the flare of anger in Marie's brown eyes and quickly held up a hand of placation. "Wait. You gotta understand something about rock-and-roll people. They like dim girls who don't talk and look pretty. Just do this little thing for me, okay?"

"Ordinarily I'd tell you to go—"

"Ah, yes, my sweet, I'm sure you would. But we live in extraordinary times, yes? Rutherford has to stay here," he said as he ushered Marie out of the car and up the winding brick path to a stained glass door that towered over both of them. He rang the bell and somewhere beyond the massive stucco wall, chimes played "Strawberry Fields Forever." Zalman cringed and looked over at Marie, who'd assumed a vacant expression with her lips parted.

"This dim enough?" she stage-whispered.

Before he could reply a voice scratched out of a speaker embedded in the wall beside the door. "Yesssss?" it queried in sepulchral tones. At the same time a large sign began to flash "Go Away!" in pink neon.

"Jerry Zalman to see Count Monty," Zalman snarled.

The door swung open slowly, complete with recorded "Inner Sanctum" sound effects and maniacal ghoulish laughter. Strobe lights flashed and booming thunder was followed by the sound of a torrential downpour. Then came recorded clanking chains and more maniacal laughter. "Follow the bouncing ball," the sepulchral voice intoned as rows of yellow globes began to blink furiously, lighting a pathway down a hall done up to look like the yellow brick road.

Still wearing her Barbie doll expression Marie said, "Gee, Mr. Zalman, this is some fun!"

"Quiet," Zalman muttered under his breath as they followed the bouncing balls down the hallway into a gigantic living room with fake stone walls where a group of stoned-looking people of indeterminate age and in some cases indeterminate sex were lying around on waterbeds, wearing headphones and watching an old Flash Gordon serial on a big projection TV. None of them noticed the two newcomers, but almost at once a tall girl with waist-length hair appeared in a doorway across the room and called, "Mr. Zalman? Over here . . ."

Zalman and Marie waded through the sea of

waterbeds to the young woman. "Hi, I'm Cassandra," she said with a vacuous smile. "C'mon in." She led the way through a stone grotto into a huge private office done in slanted strips of teak paneling, framed record company promotion art, indirect lighting, and big aquariums filled with exotic luminescent fish. In the midst of all this Count Monty rose heavily from behind a monstrous free-form redwood burl desk. "How'd you like the entrance?" he asked proudly in his famous gravelly voice. "Designed it myself."

Count Monty was absolutely huge: six-six or so, three hundred pounds, easy. He extended his hand with the stately magnificence of a Brontosaurus about to nibble a tree and shook Zalman's hand. Wordlessly, he took Marie's little hand and kissed it thoughtfully. His face was nearly covered with a thick black beard which left little to see except his eyes, which were very bright and set too close together. His hair was beginning to go on top, but to make up for the beginnings of baldness it reached to his waist. He was wearing a straining T-shirt, faded bib overalls, and a CALL GEORGE Beatles pin.

Realizing Count Monty was an unreconstructed hippie, and a rich one to boot, Zalman grinned engagingly and said, "Really dug the front door. Did it all yourself, huh?"

Count Monty resettled his bulk behind his desk. "Yup. Like the first thing you see ought to set the tone, know where I'm coming from?"

"For sure," Zalman agreed, nearly gagging. He and Marie sat down in carved wood and leather chairs, and he noted she was deep into her dim act, eyes roving around the room with the blank stare of a newly hatched moth.

"Heard you wanted to get together," Zalman said.

"Heard *you* wanted to talk to *me*," Count Monty replied evenly. He was large but he wasn't slow.

Zalman fished a Cuban cigar from his case and stared at it appraisingly. "Cigar? Mind if I smoke?" Count Monty waved a hand and shook his head. Zalman leaned back and slowly lit his cigar. "Phil Hanning," he said, "is my brother-in-law. Lucille is my sister."

Count Monty nodded sagely and so did his various rolls of fat. "You got a nice family," he offered pleasantly.

"Yeah," Zalman said, blowing smoke, "but maybe not too bright in some departments. For instance, Phil says he's involved in a financial arrangement with you, Slim Honniger, who's a close personal friend and client of mine, and with Al Hix."

Count Monty lifted his eyebrows. "Sure, we're getting together on a little thing. What do you want to know?"

"Well, with Sticky Al being the late Sticky Al and the money disappearing, I was wondering where you stood . . ."

"What!" Count Monty blurted in genuine amazement. He half rose from his chair, then realizing it was too much effort to elevate his bulk, he sank back down. "You telling me Sticky Al's like . . ."

"Dead," Zalman said slowly, studying Count Monty carefully. "You didn't know? I find that hard to believe. Don't you watch TV?"

"Nah," Monty mumbled in a daze. "It upsets my creative flow, you know where I'm coming from? I don't go out much anymore. I tape the

93

show from here. I got a full studio downstairs, everything I need, even for live hookups. I don't get the papers or anything."

Zalman inclined his head toward the living room. "None of your pals go out either?" he prodded.

Count Monty shook his head. "Bad vibes. We get everything delivered. But about Al—dead? How?"

Zalman shook his own head in wonderment at the ways of the world. "The lady and I found him parked in a refrigerator, shot. And yesterday a Mr. Downley informs me that Phil's out of the deal since it seems Al didn't deliver the front money before he so conveniently died. Guess that means you too, huh?"

Once again Count Monty was visibly shaken. "That bitch!" he sputtered. "Where does Lila get off ranking on me? If it hadn't been for my guest list she wouldn't be having any auction. I'll sue her ass."

"That's possible," Zalman said. "Listen, I believe you. You didn't know Sticky Al was spinning on that turntable in the sky. So what *do* you know?"

Count Monty stared at his Viking hall beamed ceiling, then at his collection of Day-Glo fish. "I dunno, man," he mumbled through his beard. "This shit about Al . . . maybe I ought to keep my mouth shut."

Once again Zalman raised the palm of placation. "Whatever's right," he intoned smoothly. "You're upset about Al, but you can tell me anything. Give me a retainer—then you're my client, dig? Privileged information, like. I just want to keep my sister and that jerk Phil out of trouble and maybe protect everybody's investment at the same time." Zalman grinned.

Count Monty reached for his checkbook like his life depended on it, which wasn't that far off base in Zalman's opinion. "Privileged communication, huh? Could the lady wait outside?" he asked anxiously. "No offense," he told Marie quickly.

"Run along, babe," Zalman told her, hoping Count Monty didn't catch his wink.

Marie played her part perfectly. "For sure," she said blankly. "I'll be in the Flash Gordon room." She left.

"Nice lady," Count Monty mumbled. "In touch, know what I mean?" He scribbled his John Hancock on the bottom of an embossed check and handed it across the immense desk. "That do you?" he asked.

"Very nicely," Zalman said, glancing at the check, then folding it into his pocket. "We're in business. Now tell me why a smart guy like you got himself involved in this Henderson thing."

Count Monty settled back into his throne chair. "You're an around guy. You know who I am, what I do. I've been in the L.A. music scene . . . hell, for a long time. I *was* the L.A. music scene back in the days of underground radio, when FM really stood for something." His tone was that of a man who had personally guaranteed world peace to the masses. "Okay, but I'm like a collector—music stuff, natch, nostalgia. You know what I'm talking about?"

"As a matter of fact, I do. Go on."

"A while ago I buy this piece for my collection from this certain party through Sticky Al. A few weeks later Al asks me over to the party's house to look at the whole collection. Al's real excited, says it's the buy of the century, a very large collection of music memorabilia. The lady who owns the stuff is a closet collector, one of those people who's got a lot of stuff and stashed it all away and nobody, not even dealers, knows she's got it. She lives out in Encino, big place, very high class. Seems her boyfriend split, Vinnie Scalisi—"

"Vinnie 'the Disposal'?" Zalman interrupted incredulously. "This is getting worse and worse." Vinnie "the Disposal" Scalisi was reputedly a crime-family chief with "business interests" in the hazardous waste industry—hence his nickname.

"Yeah, but that was no sweat—he wasn't around," Monty went on obliviously. "Like she doesn't have enough money anymore with Vinnie gone so she figures if she sells off most of the collection she can raise enough dough to move to Carmel and live off the interest. She's not broke, you dig? It's just that the joint in Encino costs a fortune to run and she's looking to start a new life. Get a job in an art gallery or something."

"Sounds like my ex-wife," Zalman muttered. "Both of them."

"Al needed my expertise, Jerry, so for him, plus the chance of getting in on the thing, I left the house, which is now beginning to look like a major screw-up. We went over and took a look, and I wouldn't be surprised if on the open market the collection could bring a million. You may find this hard to believe but I could use a piece of that."

Seeing Zalman's look of surprise Count Monty grinned and said sadly, "I'm not as flush as I look. In fact, I'm sort of in the same bag as this lady. I mean, this house is worth a fortune, yeah, but right now the market's in the dumper and I can't move it. Shoulda cleared out in '79 or '80 but we all make mistakes, right?"

"You want to quit the business?" Zalman asked in amazement. Count Monty was, after all, a rock-and-roll legend.

"I'm gonna be forty next time," Count Monty said dolefully. "You think a grown man wants to have hair down to his waist? No way. But I got an image to protect. I gotta look like this to deal with the creeps in the business I'm in. Christ, Jerry, I'm sick of this hair. You know how long it takes to wash? I gotta have a guy come over every day to wash my goddamn hair. I want to retire too. Move to Colorado or someplace where it snows. No more goddamn heat. Also I'm thinking of going to a weight clinic before my pump goes on me. But to tie up all the goddamn loose ends I need cash, which is why I went in with Sticky Al on this auction. I didn't figure it was gonna solve all my problems but everything helps, right?"

"You also provided the mailing list?"

"Yeah," Monty said vehemently. "The mailing list! And now that bitch wants to cut me out! It was an A list, too. Strictly your big bucks industry crowd."

"Did the invitations go out?"

"Yeah. Cassandra, the lady who let you in, she helped Al on the invites and I know they went out. The thing's supposed to go down this coming Thursday at Lila's place. Jerry, I got any legal recourse? She says she didn't get the dough but she sure as shit got my A list."

"She's sure as shit got something, Count, old buddy," Zalman said thoughtfully, chewing on his cigar. "Speaking as your attorney, I think it's time I had a little chat with this Lila Henderson."

Count Monty wrote down Lila Henderson's address on a gilt-edged card and passed it across to Zalman. "You'll be at the auction Thursday?"

Zalman hoisted himself upright. "I wouldn't miss it, pal, not for the entire world. Talk to me later."

Two minutes afterward Zalman and Marie were rocketing down the canyon in the Mercedes. "What a scene," Marie said huffily, stroking Rutherford's head. "Count Monty's pals have shit for brains."

"Curiouser and curiouser," Zalman mused. "But Monty's no dope, even if the rest of his gang are cretins."

"Al really got around, didn't he? You ask me, he got in over his head."

"Very good observation, Watson. Seems like all these guys are in over their heads. Phil Hanning's strictly peanuts. Slim Honniger's a big operator in his own way but he's a car thief, not a collector. With the exception of this Henderson dame, of course, Count Monty's the only one who knows anything about rock and roll."

"You think one of them killed Sticky Al?" she asked flatly.

"I gave up my faith in human nature when I hung up my love beads," Zalman said. "Offhand, however, I'd say no. Hanning may be a schmuck, but he's no killer. Slim or Monty, who knows what they'd do if they thought they could get away with it. But guys like that only take risks if the money's big enough, and despite Monty's poor-mouth act he's far from broke and Slim Honniger's got more money than God. But somebody killed Al, and if he got what he was looking for, which we assume was the front money, why wreck your place, not to mention mine? But if the killer didn't get what he was looking for . . . Look, you're positive Al couldn't have stashed the money at your place?"

"He was never there," Marie answered. "All he gave me was the envelope with the button."

"And each of the boys has one of those," Zalman said thoughtfully.

"I assume you're inviting me to the auction? If not, I'm going to crash, checkbook in hand."

"Of course I'm inviting you," Zalman assured her, pulling up to the light at Laurel Canyon and Hollywood Boulevard. "I'm a regular guy who never let a lady down, especially a lady who's nuts about Elvis dolls and Beatles pins." He glanced over, wondering what she was thinking.

"Why don't we go back to your place," she suggested quietly.

Zalman swung the car west up Hollywood Boulevard and ten minutes later they pulled into his driveway. The house was cool and quiet, the curtains drawn tight against the encroaching sunlight of the late afternoon. Isobel had done her best but as usual, her best wasn't half good enough. She'd made some desultory attempts to right the wreckage of the previous evening. Most of the furniture had been put back more or less in its original position but everything was tilted the wrong way, chairs faced the wall, and the sofa, which she'd clumsily sewn together with great looping stitches of red woolen yarn, looked like a badly wrapped Christmas present.

"Jesus," Zalman moaned, thinking of the enormous bills he'd face from his decorator. Marie touched a soft hand to his lips.

"Don't worry about it now," she said, caressing his cheek. "Let's not worry about anything for a little while." She kissed him lightly on the mouth and went through the living room, the bedroom, and into the dressing room. Through the open door he saw her slip out of her clothes and lower her lush little body into the burbling hot tub.

He felt a tremendous thrill run over him as he saw her settle into the water and lean her head back on the tiles. Rutherford whined and nipped playfully at his legs. "Shut up, you filthy cur," Zalman muttered as he threw his jacket on the floor. "You wreck this for me and I'll have your head for a handball." He tossed the rest of his clothes on the floor behind him and got into the tub beside Marie.

"Mmmmmm, this is swell, Mr. Attorney," she whispered as he began to caress her. "I think I'm going to enjoy this."

"Trust me." He grinned. "I guarantee it."

They made love in the tub, got out, dried off, and had a glass of cold wine in the kitchen. Rutherford had apparently heeded Zalman's warning; the dog was fast asleep on the couch, growling pitifully at a dream cat that was just out of his reach.

Then Zalman and Marie went back to bed and made love again and fell asleep wrapped in each other's arms like a pair of animals in a litter. When they woke it was dark outside and Rutherford was sleeping on the end of the bed. Zalman pulled open the curtains and they finished the wine and watched Hollywood light up beneath them with all the glitter of the Fourth of July.

"Now, Jerry," she said, "tell me how it is that

a kid from the picket lines ended up as the pride of Beverly Hills, hmmmm? I mean, I look around, I see a guy on the up-o-later, a guy with Dunhill clocks and Gucci socks. What happened to your ideals?"

"I have plenty of ideals," he said defensively. "I'm still a member of the ACLU! It's just that times got hard in the eighties. Jesus"—he shivered—"can you imagine what the nineties are going to be like? You gotta look out for yourself!"

"Sure, sure," she mocked. "Caviar shortages, guys selling IBM stock on street corners, buddy can you spare a few thou for a cup of cappuccino —bloody frightening!"

Zalman bit her gently on the shoulder. "That's for having a smart mouth," he said. "Listen, I got tired of being poor. One day my car blew up on the goddamn Santa Monica Freeway at rush hour and I was standing there in the ninety-five-degree heat eating hot smog and I realized that poverty and Jerry Zalman can't dance, know what I mean? Your dad had just sent my pal McCoy to jail and you know, it sorta put the fear of God into me. Now McCoy, he's eight feet tall and he's got tattoos and he knows how to chew up nails and spit out tacks, if you catch my drift. But suddenly, standing there on the freeway, I got this picture of myself trying to negotiate my way out of a just-best-friends relationship with some monster in San Q and I knew that prison wasn't for me. Didn't fit into my future. Neither did having a fifteen-year-old Chevy blow up on you and there you are standing in the parking lot at the 7-Eleven wishing to hell you could afford to have the Triple A come and tow the junker out into the goddamn ocean and deep-six it instead of standing there like a stooge waiting for your dumb brother-in-law to come and pick you up and help you push the Chevy down the freeway. I decided to get rich." Zalman grinned happily. "I still got ideals, doll," he said. "I'm a capitalist."

Marie hooted with laughter. "You're a regular Dave del Dotto, Jerry. Seven E-Z steps to Wealth and Prosperity."

"Listen, doll, there's more than seven and it ain't easy."

"You oughta tape this and sell it to schoolkids. It's very inspirational."

"Enough of this insouciant chitchat," he said brightly. "You hungry?"

"Ravenous. Want to eat here or go out?"

He laughed. "I don't think there's any food here. Maybe some canned soup, a couple eggs. I always eat out."

"Always? Where?" she asked, turning on her side so she could look at him. Rutherford snuggled in between them and she stroked his sleek fur.

"Usually in the morning I go to Manya's Yummy or maybe Finest Snax out in the Valley if I have business, or Nate 'n Al's in Beverly Hills. Lunch I usually have at Le Croque because it's close to my office and very easy. Dinner I always eat out with a client or a lady if I'm entertaining. Sunday I go to my sister's house for brisket. In between I order from Greenblatt's or pick up something from Ah Fong's."

"Sounds like a lot of cholesterol," she teased. "So where do you want to eat?"

He glanced at the Dunhill clock, which fortunately the intruder hadn't smashed. It was seven o'clock. "I'll call Le Croque," he said. "Maybe some lamb chops would go good right now." He picked up the phone, dialed, and told the girl they'd be there in an hour. "Then we'll come back here and—"

"Not tonight, dear." She giggled. "I have to wash my hair."

"Already it starts," he moaned in mock horror. "And here I was going to show you my *Out of the Past* tape."

An hour later they strolled into Le Croque and found the joint jumping. Pierre led Zalman and Marie to a table near the bar. "Not zee usual," Pierre mumbled apologetically, "but on zee short notice—"

"No problem, Pete," Zalman assured him, waving at a willowy blonde he thought he recognized from the hazy days after his last divorce. "We came to eat."

"I feel self-conscious," Marie whispered after Pierre had settled her in her chair and bustled away. "I don't think I'm dressed for this place." She had borrowed one of Zalman's blue shirts and left it open to the waist, then knotted it so that although nothing was seen everything was suggested. She was wearing jeans and her penny loafers, and the effect was of a depraved sub-deb of the 1950s.

"Nobody with a décolletage like yours has any reason to feel self-conscious," Zalman told her. "Quite zee contraire."

"Zally," a familiar voice panted anxiously behind him. "How goes it?"

Zalman did not turn around. "Get away from

me, Phil, you lying weasel," he said pleasantly. "You're supposed to be under house arrest, and if I see your chiseling face this evening I'll tear you limb from limb, I swear on the life of this innocent young girl beside me."

Phil Hanning clapped his brother-in-law on the back and sat down next to Marie. "Phil Hanning," he said, pumping her paw. He turned to Zalman. "Any news? Whaddya find out? Huh, Zally?"

"Couldn't you have told the truth for once in your useless life?" Zalman asked as he signaled for service. "I drove all over the city just to find out what you know already. Bullshot for me," he told the waiter, "white wine for the lady, and a cup of hemlock for the gentleman. Make that a double."

Hanning laughed hollowly and tugged at the collar of his pink-and-black silk shirt as if it were a noose. "Zally, you gotta great sense of humor."

Zalman lit a cigar and stared pointedly around the room. "Lucille's not here? I want to speak to her about taking you to the vet and having you put to sleep. Except for the fact that I've met this charming lady, the last two days have been a dead waste, Phil. And you are responsible."

Hanning shifted nervously in his chair, grabbed Marie's water glass, and drained it. "Zally, c'mon, don't kid me. What about the DeLorean?"

"Ah-hah! Another lie! I spoke to Slim Honniger and he's going to hold onto the car. As a personal favor to me. Got it? Now I owe him. But no car till I get this mess straightened out, Phil. Now get out of here before I decide to commit mayhem." Zalman turned to Marie. "Know what the legal definition of *mayhem* is?" he asked.

"No." She giggled. "But I bet you're going to tell me."

"The willful and permanent crippling, mutilation, or disfigurement of a person," Zalman recited. "Like I chopped off one of Phil's arms and then beat him over the head with it, that would count as mayhem. Not the beating over the head—I guess that would be assault. The arm-chopping, though, that would be mayhem."

"I get it. You guys want to be alone?" Hanning said, rising hastily. "Okay, lovebirds, I can take a hint. So we'll talk later, huh, Zally?" he asked as he faded into the crowd around the bar.

"Yes, Phil, talk to me later," Zalman said wearily.

In comparison, the rest of the evening was easy. Zalman had his broiled lamb chops with a good Burgundy and a green salad enhanced by Pierre's cucumber dressing. Marie had sole and an artichoke which Pierre swore had been flown in from Castroville that very morning. Zalman told a few jokes which Marie insisted she'd never heard before, and she told him about how it felt to grow up the daughter of a cop.

"It was strange when I was a kid," she said as she daintily skinned an artichoke leaf. "Nobody else's dad packed a gun around the house. He never took it off." She laughed and shook her head ruefully. "I remember one time we were having a barbecue—it was my twelfth birthday—and my dad was wearing this apron that said 'Hot Dawg!' on it and a chef's hat and madras Bermuda shorts and a .38."

"Barney Miller takes his gun off when he

comes home," Zalman offered. "He has a whole ritual about the bullets in one place and gun in another."

Marie shook her head. "Not Arnold Thrasher. Nosireebob. Kept it right on his hip and loaded, except when he slept, and then it went under his pillow. Sure made you feel safe, though—kind of like having John Wayne around all the time."

"Tell me," Zalman asked, "did he ever shoot anybody?"

Marie laughed. "Nope."

"The prosecution rests," Zalman said. "Want dessert?"

"Sure, I want dessert. What's good?"

Zalman motioned for the dessert cart, and Marie chose a Napoleon and a chocolate truffle. Zalman had a brandy. "Zelnick was right. You've certainly got a healthy appetite," he remarked. "Does your mother run to fat?"

Marie nearly choked on her truffle. "Skinny and beautiful," she said, sticking out her chocolaty tongue. "So there!"

Zalman ordered a hamburger to go for Rutherford in a little box, complete with a pink silk Le Croque napkin; then they went outside and kissed a few times while they stood around waiting for the car. He thought how nice it was to know a girl who could talk about something other than her latest audition. The fact that she liked to neck in parking lots was an added bonus. A little breeze was blowing and Zalman opened the sun roof as they drove back to his house. This time their lovemaking was slower, sweeter . . .

"Can I tell you something that's going to sound a little Freudian?" Zalman asked. It was now close to three in the morning. Zalman, Marie, and Rutherford were lying in bed, listening to jazz on the radio. Zalman was smoking a cigar, Marie was nestled in his arms, and Rutherford had eaten his hamburger and was hanging off the end of the bed in an imitation of a self-satisfied vulture.

"Freudian?" Marie asked. "It's not going to be something that entails rubber, I hope."

Zalman ignored her. "You sort of remind me of my sister. Understand," he added hurriedly, "that I do not do this with my sister."

"Not even when you were kids?" she teased, reaching across him for some Perrier. "Who'd you play doctor with?"

"Louanne Springle from across the street." He grinned. "She knew some pretty good experiments, as I recall. But definitely not my sister."

"Since I have a Girl Scout merit badge in psychiatry, I assume you're telling me you feel emotionally comfortable in this current situation? Is that close?" she asked. "Tell me, Herr Patient, is it unusual for you to feel comfortable with women when you're in bed with them?"

"Yup"—he grinned—"since you ask. I admit that most of the girls I've known aren't exactly Rhodes scholar material."

"Are we talking airbrains here? Or just ladies with a burning desire to marry money? Or what?" Marie began to stroke Rutherford with her foot, and the dog stretched out along the full length of the bed and made swimming motions with his feet.

Zalman lay silent, smoking his cigar. The soft wind through the open window blew the curtains into the room, and somewhere across the canyon a coyote howled fitfully. The huge city seemed unnaturally quiet.

"I really don't know," he said frankly. "I'm a two-time winner myself—twice divorced. But hell, I can't blame it all on the girls. I didn't really want to get married but the girls did and I was tired of driving back and forth to their apartments to feed their cats and coming home at weird hours to change clothes and, besides, both of them liked Chinese food. What more could a guy ask for?"

Marie shifted on her side and reached out for his cigar. She took a ladylike puff and regarded him meditatively. "A guy could ask for true love, couldn't he? So could a lady. But love is tough to find in these perilous times. Used to be you couldn't get good Chinese food, but you could manage to stay married to the same person most of your life. Now we got Chinese, Cajun, Philippine, any kind of cuisine you like. But everybody's divorced. I thought I liked my ex-husband pretty well. I thought he liked *me* pretty well. He's a chef. Taught me all I know about food. We got married after he taught me to cook carnitas. After a year I found out he was having a thing with one of his sous chefs, pretty girl who was seriously into black bean sauce. I forgave him. God, was I noble! Then he did it again. This time I wasn't so forgiving."

"How long ago was this?" Zalman asked, taking his cigar back.

"Let's see . . . six years. Afterward I got a job at ABC in the typing pool. I have a master's degree in English, can you believe it? Two years later I realized that if I didn't do something I was going to end up as one of those movie studio dragon lady secretaries who drink too much at lunch and have yappy little dogs. No offense, Rutherford. I had to make a living, and I sure wasn't going to sit around with the blinds drawn and the electric blanket turned up to nine on the weekends like some of my girlfriends. I noticed how much work we were sending out to independent typing joints so I decided to go into business for myself. End of the story of Marie's life. Now you have it all."

"We'll see about that," Zalman said mischievously, nuzzling her neck. "You're right, though," he said thoughtfully. "I think what I really mean is that Lucille is the only woman I trust. Actually, she's the only woman I really know. Oh sure, she's a pain in the ass sometimes but . . ."

". . . she's the only woman you take seriously," Marie prompted.

He trimmed the glowing tip off his cigar and rolled toward her. "Yeah," he said. "Until recently."

In the morning they lazed around the house and Marie cooked an old-fashioned eggs and toast breakfast. They tried to straighten up a few things, Marie took a soak in the hot tub, and Zalman swam a few laps in the pool while Rutherford barked playfully at him from the patio. Later, Zalman urged Marie to stay on at his house for the time being. He made the suggestion more for romantic than security reasons, although they were both uncomfortably aware the ransacker was still at large, and Marie consented, more for romantic than security reasons. They made phone calls to their respective places of business and issued instructions for the day; then Marie phoned Greenblatt's and ordered a raft of food including lox, bagels, pumpernickel bread, and three kinds of cheese. She also raided his cellar for champagne.

"You always cook like this?" he asked, hovering on the edges of his kitchen, watching her arrange the food buffet-style on a silver platter. "If this goes on I'm going to take up jogging or something equally mindless."

"I'll give you something mindless," Marie said with a sidelong glance. "Here, make yourself useful." She handed him the platter and they went out onto the patio.

"Jesus." Zalman sighed as he leaned back in his chair after lunch. "I feel like a Strasbourg goose."

"To eat is to live." She laughed. "Have some more, Jerry. This is the first flower of our romance. Can't we throw cholesterol to the winds and spend the day in the kitchen? And in bed, of course?" She gave Rutherford another buttered bagel and he wolfed it happily.

"I'd like to," he admitted. "But I've got to go see Lila Henderson."

"Lila Henderson!" she squealed. "You fink! And here I thought you were smitten with moi. Ah well"—she sighed melodramatically—"men are fickle things after all."

"Strictly business, I swear it on the heads of our unborn children." He raised a hand in mock salute.

"That's better, then." She grinned. "Cross your heart you're not going to pork her?"

"Pork!" He laughed incredulously. "Pork! My dear young woman, I do not 'pork.' I may sweep a woman off her feet in a whirlwind of passion. I may drive her mad in a wild frenzy of desire. But I do not 'pork.' As you ought to know. Actually," Zalman said with a wicked gleam in his eye, "I plan to threaten the lady's ass, not jump on it."

LILA HENDERSON LIVED IN THE HEART OF THE San Fernando Valley on a choice piece of real estate in Encino, a few blocks south of Ventura Boulevard. The house was a large white brick building that looked like it had started out to be Colonial, had moved into Ranch, and ended up California. Bougainvillea climbed the walls, English ivy wound its lazy way up and down a pair of trellises next to the front door, and graceful poplars waved over the cedar shake roof. The effect was rich but not plush.

The front door opened and Chuck Downley smiled sweetly. "Ah, Mr. Zalman. How nice. I thought you'd turn up sooner or later. How's your charming brother-in-law?" His thin fingers drummed nervously on the doorframe.

Zalman smiled and raised the famed hand of placation. "Phil's sorry he was rude, Chuck. He was overwrought. He wants to forget the incident and I'm sure you do too."

"What makes you think that?" Downley asked, looking decidedly grumpy. "I'm still thinking lawsuit."

"Well, Chuck, old sport," Zalman said smoothly, "you do whatever you want, but I'd say your chances are about zero. There's no witness to the alleged incident. It's your word against Mr.

Hanning's. And speaking as his lawyer I'll see to it you pick up the court costs when you lose." Zalman smiled again, showing his teeth this time. "Now, tell Lila I'm here."

Downley glared at him, fuming. "I'll see if Ms. Henderson's in . . . to you," he said in arctic tones, shutting the door in Zalman's face.

Zalman chuckled under his breath, jingled his Gucci key ring, and admired the ivy. A moment later Downley was back, still fuming but in better control. "She says okay," he announced. "Follow me." He led the way around the side of the house on a herringbone brick path lined with full, old-fashioned roses and hanging baskets of fat fuchsias dripping purple blossoms. The path emptied onto a huge flagstone patio that faced a large swimming pool. Chairs and glass-topped tables were scattered about casually, and a light breeze rippled the water in the big pool. It was very quiet and private. Aside from the sleepy droning of bees the only sound was the smooth, well-oiled purr of the pool heater's motor.

"Over here!" a voice trilled. Zalman turned and saw Lila Henderson in a corner of the garden, standing next to one of the deep flower beds, cardboard pots of transplants and garden tools at her feet. She was wearing a tiny bikini and a huge straw hat with veils that made her look like the deranged keeper of the bees cruising her garden. "Bring some drinks, Chuckie."

"Chuckie . . . ?" Zalman needled in an undertone.

"Drop dead," Downley huffed, then wheeled away toward the house.

"Well, hi there!" Lila warbled, coming toward him, removing gloves and hat, and Zalman saw

113

she had the biggest pair of baby blues this side of Carol Channing. She looked about forty. Her hair was an artful burnished gold, but the skimpy bikini proved her figure was in mint condition. Aside from the bikini her only other article of attire was a simple little diamond ring that looked like it had last seen duty on the front of a locomotive. Zalman also noted her height; she was at least six feet, a perfect specimen of the leggy showgirl type he invariably went for.

Zalman kissed Lila's hand. "Ms. Henderson," he said warmly. "I'm Jerry Zalman, Phil Hanning's brother-in-law and Slim Honniger's and Count Monty's lawyer. I've been wanting to meet you, to suggest we try to work out this misunderstanding about the auction. Yes? It's always sad when partners have a falling out, don't you think?"

Lila Henderson's little brow knitted in a perfect imitation of a human being trying to think. She shrugged helplessly, threw her gardening gloves on the table, and sank into a wrought-iron patio chair. "I don't think they're my partners anymore."

"No?" Zalman said with a touch of harshness just to see if he could make her twitch. "I'm sorry to hear you're taking this attitude."

But Lila didn't blink. "Why, honey," she trilled, "when the boys didn't come across with the money they promised me, I just figured they didn't want to be bothered with my old auction." She shook her golden head. "And then Chuckie was very upset the other day when Mr. Hanning was so mean to him. He said some awful things, and Chuckie's very sensitive." Downley reappeared, deposited a silver tray of Mimosas on a glass table, then vanished into the house.

"You've still got Count Monty's mailing list, however," Zalman pressed in a medium-nasty voice.

Lila looked at him shrewdly, and suddenly Zalman saw she wasn't a dumb blonde at all. "That's between me and Monty," she said flatly.

"I'm Monty's lawyer. So talk to me."

"It's between friends," Lila stalled. "Tell him to call me and we'll talk."

Zalman shook his head and smiled unpleasantly. "You're not receiving me. You've abrogated an agreement with my clients and you are in possession of property belonging to one of my clients, namely the list. You try to proceed without my clients' participation, you'll find yourself facing an injunction. You receiving me now?"

Lila sipped her Mimosa and regarded him coolly but not belligerently. "Look, Jerry," she said evenly, "my boyfriend and I broke up and I'm having a garage sale, that's all. I need the money so Chuckie and I can move to Carmel and live the good life, like in *Town & Country*."

Zalman decided to switch tactics too. "Look, Lila," he said intimately, "I'm not out to make life unbearable for you. I'm sure we can work something out."

They sat in silence for a couple of beats, sipping their drinks and studying each other. Finally they smiled across the table. "Too bad you don't have trunks," Lila said at last, through a sly smile. "We could have a dip in the pool."

"Another time perhaps," Zalman said easily. "Listen, Lila, up to now everybody's been a little evasive with me. How'd you come by all this stuff anyway?"

She took a healthy swig of her drink and

laughed harshly. "You may not believe this, Jerry, but twenty years ago I was quite the rock-and-roll cutie. I was living in San Francisco when Flower Power hit big, and let me tell you that city went nuts. I was with this guy at the time who was a DJ. Matter of fact, Monty sort of reminds me of him a little bit, except my guy was all skin and bones. Well anyway, he was big then and, Jesus, those record company guys used to load him up with all this promo material. Those days anybody with long hair could get their butts signed. The record company guys were all nudnicks in suits, didn't know what this crazy music was." She laughed dreamily, took another slug of Mimosa, and sighed.

"And then what happened?" Zalman coaxed with professional expertise.

"Uh yeah, well," Lila continued, "he used to bring home all this stuff and I kept it. T-shirts and posters and dolls and perfume bottles and God knows what all, and when we broke up and I moved down here I took the stuff with me. Then I got involved with a musician and people gave him stuff too and eventually, when he hit it big, record guys knew I collected stuff so they put me on their distribution lists, hoping to score points with my boyfriend. And so on and so on. The stuff just kept piling up."

Lila Henderson smiled her Cheshire cat smile, making an inventory in her mind. "I have every poster Mouse ever did," she said. "All the Fillmore concerts in San Francisco, I have. Comic books? Crumb, naturally. Bob Williams. Trina Robbins, I got it all. Albums? I have every album, every single that was made between, oh, 1962 and, hell, a few years ago, I guess. Original art? No problem. Stuff from record companies the art directors used to send me. Later on, I'd buy stuff. It's a fabulous collection if I say so myself, and I do . . ." She trailed off as a faraway look filled her baby blues.

"How did you meet Sticky Al?" Zalman asked, hoping to get the conversation back on a more manageable plane.

"Vinnie Scalisi, my ex-boyfriend," she explained, watching Zalman to see if the name registered. "Vinnie likes to gamble and sometimes Al booked bets for him—ran messages, more like. Al was a real small-timer but Vinnie liked him and kept him around for company sometimes. Vinnie thinks he's an upscale guy and maybe Al reminded him of the old days before the Scalisis started reading *Gentleman's Quarterly*. I don't know. Anyhow, after Vinnie and I broke up Al called and wanted to know if I was interested in selling a certain piece from the collection. He said he could arrange a buyer and heard I was strapped for cash—"

"I find that hard to believe," Zalman interrupted, gesturing with his glass at the big house and garden.

"Oh, that." Lila snorted. "It's a lease, in my name. Vinnie won't sign anything so now I'm stuck with the damned rent and upkeep, and it's breaking me."

"You were saying . . ."

Lila's huge eyes misted over with tears. "It was a jacket that belonged to Elvis, one of his show jackets. He'd given it to me personally, had it sent over actually after I'd been to one of his Vegas dates. I was with Les, my musician boyfriend, and we went backstage. Les wasn't even sure Elvis would remember him, but he did."

Lila breathed and wiped at her nose with a napkin. She fell silent for a moment, her dreamy eyes focused on faraway stars. "Elvis remembered Les and he kissed me on the cheek. He was so nice . . . We got to talking and I mentioned I collected rock-and-roll memorabilia and said I had some of his early 45s, some E.P. Enterprises stuff. He laughed and said he'd make sure I got something better than that. Well, a few days later a limo pulls up in front of the house and the driver brings in a package and it's one of Elvis's jackets! I hated like hell to part with it, but Monty paid top dollar. He was the buyer, of course." She looked sad for a moment longer, then brightened. "Well, no more tears for Elvis," she said wryly.

"And then Al put the auction together?" Zalman prompted.

"About a month later he said he could get the whole thing up, that Monty had a dynamite mailing list of big spenders and they'd give me thirty thousand in front for fifteen points. Hell, I jumped at it. Sure, I know I could make more doing it on my own, but I'm not greedy. All I want is to get me and Chuckie out of L.A., but I'm out of touch these days. The only people I know are Vinnie's friends and the girls at the gym, and they don't know a Mouse poster from a paper bag. I may look like Miss Snazz but basically I just want to play with my plants." She tapped a gold-nailed finger against her temple meaningfully. "Too much fast lane. Can't handle the pace anymore." She laughed and her voice had the gritty crunch of gravel on a driveway.

Zalman felt he was getting a look at another side of Lila Henderson, the real Lila who lived beneath the dumb-blonde act, the rock-and-roll cutie, as she'd put it, the mobster's girlfriend —and the essential Lila was no dope. She was a survivor and he was forced to wonder if she'd had anything to do with Sticky Al's untimely departure or the burglaries. He figured she was capable of just about anything. She wasn't a monster, just very tough, and in Zalman's book that made her prime suspect material. As he'd told Marie, he didn't figure Slim or Monty for the villain since the gain wasn't worth the risk for guys in their tax brackets, and Phil Hanning was neither smart nor tough enough to be the bad guy—besides, he just didn't have a killer's instinct. But if Zalman was any judge of character, and he was, Lila Henderson was in firm possession of all those factors and qualities. He finished his Mimosa and watched the breeze skitter leaves across the surface of the big swimming pool.

"But no money up front"—Lila's voice cut in on his thoughts—"no deal. Frankly, I don't think Monty's mailing list is worth a partnership to the rest of the boys. Hell, I'll give Monty ten grand for his part in the deal but no percentage. That's the best I can do."

"Is that a bona fide offer?" Zalman asked. "'Cause if it is, I'll ask him about it. Don't think he'll go for it, though."

"You mean *you* won't go for it," she said shrewdly. "Sure. Make him the offer. But unless I get the front money I was promised before tomorrow, that's the best I'm gonna do and I'll see the boys in court. Tell 'em that for me."

Zalman stood up. "Can I use your phone?"

"Of course," Lila said. She led the way inside the house.

"You've done a lot with this place," Zalman said, looking around, and a lot was more than enough. Lila's gigantic living room was jammed with heavy Spanish furniture, dark paintings in gilt frames, ugly bronze sculpture, and a hungry jungle of evil-looking tropical plants. The wet bar, to which Lila led him, was done in a contrasting nautical motif. There was a large display of knots framed over the bar, and coiled rope edged the bar stools, the shelves over the back bar, and the bar itself. Tiny bits of coiled rope served as coasters.

"Nautical but nice," Zalman observed. "We get sailor hats with this?"

Lila laughed. "It's on the bar," she said, pointing to a phone next to a lamp in the shape of a mermaid with a very large bosom. She walked out of the room.

He sat down on a rope-trimmed stool and dialed Esther at the office. "Hi, kid," he said. "Just to let you know I'm still on the planet. What's new in your corner?"

"Oh, Mr. Z., I'm so glad you called!" Esther gushed happily. "Lucille's called about twelve times. She's really getting crazy about the De-Lorean."

"Oh Christ, I forgot all about the damn car. Didn't she rent something?"

"She borrowed Bland's Rolls but it's got right-hand drive and I wish you'd just call her, Mr. Z. Honestly, she's driving me nuts. Pleeeese. She's at home."

"Okay, okay, I'll call her. Damn car . . . anything else?"

"McCoy tracked down Mrs. Al. She's back at her place in Thousand Oaks. He's got the house

120

staked out so he's waiting for you." She rattled off Sticky Al's address in Thousand Oaks.

"That's great," Zalman said. "If McCoy calls back, tell him to hang in there and I'll be up as soon as I can. If Mrs. Al skedaddles again, McCoy should stay with her and check in when he can—got that? Now, what else?"

Esther reeled off a list of calls, some from girls, some from clients, and Zalman told her how to handle them. "I'm gonna be busy for a few days, Esther," Zalman told her, "so I'm depending on you to cover for me. Tell everyone I've got the flu or something, will you?"

"Oh sure, Mr. Z.," she warbled. "No problem. They won't miss you anyway."

"Don't say that, Esther," he chided her, only half joking, "or you won't be going to La Costa. I'll check with you later." He hung up and dialed Lucille at home. Phil Hanning answered and after minimal conversation he put Lucille on the line.

"Zally, where's my car!" Lucille whined. "You promised you'd get it back for me. Zally, you promised! I don't want anybody else driving it. You go get it yourself. No messenger service, okay? Bland loaned me his car but it's got right-hand drive and I hate it and it scares me. Please, Zally . . ."

Zalman sighed and stared out Lila Henderson's mullioned window at the big pool, lit to a brilliant aqua by the brilliant sky. Palm trees waved softly in the distance and the pool heater motor purred in the background, making him sleepy.

"Quit bitching, Lucille!" he barked, snapping out of his dreamy mood. "I'll go get the damned car, for God's sake!" Zalman hung up, disgruntled. Lucille and her goddamn DeLorean . . . Phil and his goddamn deals . . . He couldn't keep Marie out of his thoughts either. Somewhere in the back of the house a screen door banged, but otherwise Lila's place was pin-droppingly still. Zalman sighed and punched up Slim Honniger's number.

"Slimbo!" he said heartily when Slim's laconic secretary finally connected them. "Look, pal, no more kidding around. I gotta get the DeLorean from you, okay?" Zalman let it hang there, waiting to see which way Slim was going to jump.

"Phil gonna make good on it?" Slim Honniger asked flatly. "Or are you?"

"Don't play games with me, Slim," Zalman warned in a pleasant tone. "Like I told you, trust me. Besides, if your ex-wife should happen to find out the true extent of your assets . . ."

"Okay, okay," Slim said quickly, forcing a nervous laugh. "Send somebody for the car. It's out in back in the storage lot but I'll have it brought up front. Seriously, Jerry, somebody's in for the dough, right?"

"Sure, what else?" Zalman said wearily. "Look, I'll be down to get it myself later this afternoon. My sister fears that if anybody but a blood relative drives her car the world as we know it will crumble. See you later."

He hung up as Lila came back into the room, blond hair spread out around her creamy shoulders, her statuesque figure resplendent. Chuck Downley hovered anxiously behind her.

"Not too bad for pushing forty, huh?" Lila grinned, catching Zalman's glance.

"Too bad we had to meet under such . . . strained circumstances," Zalman said suavely, kissing her hand again. "I'll have a chat with the boys and we'll see where we are. But remember, unless we get this worked out you can figure on a deputy sheriff showing up with an injunction tomorrow." Zalman released her hand and shrugged helplessly.

"Talk it over with Monty," Lila countered, "and we'll see where we stand. No hard feelings, I hope?"

"None at all," Zalman called, heading for the door, Downley on his heels like a little terrier. "Talk to me later."

Forty-five minutes later Zalman spotted McCoy hunched down behind the wheel of a bashed-in, dirty white Datsun two-door that wouldn't have attracted notice if it were the last vehicle on the planet. He was parked in a seedy tract neighborhood on the outskirts of Thousand Oaks, about half a block down the street from the address Esther had reeled off. As Zalman cruised by he saw McCoy's eyes flicker over him like a sleepy bird's, then wander off. Zalman knew the Mercedes didn't project the right image for the neighborhood so he parked farther down the street, then walked back to the Datsun and slid into the passenger's seat.

The little car was littered with cigarette butts, crushed Styrofoam take-out coffee cups, and a few empty beer bottles. "Jesus," Zalman muttered, making a mental note to send his suit to the cleaners.

McCoy took a long drag off his cigarette, then blew the smoke out the window in deference to

Zalman's health habits and crushed the butt in the already brimming ashtray. "Took you long enough." He grinned. "What you been up to?"

"None of your damned business," Zalman said sharply. "What are you, 'Dear Abby'?"

"Yep. That Marie's a nice girl. Too damn good for you, Jerry."

"What about Mrs. Al?" Zalman snarled.

"Sure, she's in there." McCoy pointed at a run-down house catty-corner across the street. It looked like a sad place. Paint was peeling, the yard was a disaster area, and a car that could have been the twin of McCoy's filthy Datsun sagged in the oil-stained driveway. "According to the neighbor lady," McCoy drawled, "Mrs. Al and the kid showed up late last night."

As McCoy spoke a tall redhead in skin-tight shorts and a halter top came out of the house next to Mrs. Al's, waved animatedly in McCoy's general direction, adjusted a lawn sprinkler, displaying an ample amount of flank in the process, then waved again furiously and went back inside. McCoy unscrewed the top from a bottle of warm Coke and took a swig.

"Neighbor lady?" Zalman inquired innocently.

"Name of Lurlene," McCoy said blandly. "She's a cosmetologist in Camarillo, up to the state hospital. She gives the loonies beauty treatments. She was telling me Charlie Parker used to be a guest out there. Did you know that, Jerry?" He screwed the top on the Coke and tossed it in the back seat.

"Jesus," Zalman muttered again, opening the door. "Let's go see Mrs. Al." McCoy hoisted his big frame out of the little car and followed Zalman across the street.

The lawn around the Hix house was brown and littered with kids' toys. A hose was dribbling water on a stunted banana tree, but it looked like the tree was beyond hope. The screen over the front door was torn and rusty, the mailbox hung open like a gaping mouth, and Zalman felt once again he should have bought more stuff off Sticky Al.

"What is it?" a shrill woman's voice demanded before Zalman had a chance to knock.

Zalman stepped back, startled, then smiled at the closed door. "Mrs. Hix? I'm Jerry Zalman. I was your husband's lawyer," he said, lying. "There's some unfinished legal business, Mrs. Hix. I thought you'd want to go over his papers." Zalman coughed, forcing himself to go on. "His estate . . ."

There was a short silence while the closed door considered, followed by a wheezing laugh that quickly deteriorated into a coughing fit. "Estate, my Aunt Fanny!" the voice shrilled. "Al didn't have no damn estate. Whatcha want?"

Zalman sighed and flashed his engaging grin at the invisible Mrs. Al. "It's about money, Mrs. Hix," he said brightly.

Fifteen minutes later Zalman was perched uncomfortably on a ripped La-Z-Boy sipping unadulterated Lipton's instant and trying to look like he was enjoying himself. McCoy, who'd opted for the Hawaiian Punch, was sprawled on the floor watching Robot Monster cartoons with Al's eight-year-old kid, a rather sweet-faced little blond girl. The kid was hanging all over McCoy but he didn't seem to mind.

"Sure I disappeared," Gladys Hix shouted over the kitchenette bar separating the cramped kitchen from the cramped living room. She was a raddled blonde in her midthirties who might have been girlishly pretty once upon a time. Right now she was cooking a skillet of franks and canned beans, and the thick, oily smoke and aroma made Zalman slightly nauseated. "I came home from the police deal the night Al got it and the house was a wreck. I mean tore apart. Everything turned over, smashed, furniture cut up. I got scared and Allie and me got out of here, I can tell you, up to Ventura to my sister's. We came back yesterday. Took me most of the day to try and straighten up," she said, looking around halfheartedly. "Not that it's much now."

"Was anything taken?" Zalman asked.

"Hell, I don't know," Gladys shouted, flipping the franks. "Didn't take the TV or radio or my high school graduation pearls so I don't guess he was much of a burglar. If I'da caught the guy searching the place I woulda offered to help him look and anything we found, we'd split it. Nah, Al wasn't what you call a good provider. But I'll tell you what I think, Mr. Zalman, I think it had something to do with Al. Oh sure, I know about his little schemes. He didn't tell me nothing, but that don't mean he put anything over on me either. I think he was into something and somebody thought something was hid out here. That's what I think," she said with finality, giving the franks a nasty jab with her spatula.

"You share your theory with the police yet?" Zalman inquired.

"Hell no! I don't have nothing more to do with cops than necessary. That's my motto. I always knew Al was gonna get in a wringer one day. I always said, 'Al, you think you can get away with anything but you can't!' That's what I always said," she testified vehemently, her heavily mascaraed eyes filling with tears. "I just thank the good Lord little Allie was next door with Lurlene when the house got wrecked. I don't know what I'd do if my little baby got hurt." Gladys sniffed. Zalman knew she was on the verge of bawling.

"Look, Mrs. Hix, I know this is painful to talk about," he interjected quickly before the waterworks got started. "But did Al do anything unusual lately? Did he say anything unusual or do anything out of the ordinary? Try and remember. It could be important."

"Nah, nothing," Gladys said flatly. "We broke up—again—a few weeks back and I kicked his ass out—again. About all that happened after that was he showed up one day with a buncha weenies. You know, franks." She speared one out of the skillet with a fork and held it up for Zalman's inspection. "Didn't tell me where he got 'em but he didn't have to. I knew they was stolen. Everything Al had was stolen. One time he got half a truckload of franks and two sides of beef off this guy, hadda rent a meat locker downtown and everything. I figured the same deal came around again and that's how come Al had the two cases of weenies he brought us." She sighed. "There's only so many ways to fix weenies . . ."

Shortly thereafter Zalman and Gladys Hix ran out of conversation, and he and McCoy drove back to L.A. separately. Zalman felt distinctly unhappy during the trip. Ever since the night Captain Arnold Thrasher had not-so-subtly threatened him with Sticky Al's murder, Zalman had prayed and hoped that Mrs. Al would provide a lead pointing to the real killer. She'd been his only hope, but now, after talking with her, Zalman felt instinctively she didn't know any more about Al's demise than he did. It was disheartening. Zalman had a healthy respect for Arnold Thrasher's malice and didn't want to test it any further than he already had. He wanted to provide Thrasher with a solid lead that would steer the big cop off in another direction, but now Zalman had a very uncomfortable feeling he'd be hearing from Thrasher all too soon.

With this ugly thought nibbling at his mind he slipped through a window in traffic and made it back to his office in record time. But when he pulled the Mercedes into the underground parking garage below his building he saw another, more immediate problem waiting for him. A long black limousine with tinted glass was blocking his parking space, and as he pulled up two young men in well-cut sharkskin suits got out of the big car and came over to him.

"You Mr. Zalman?" the shorter of the two asked.

Zalman nodded. "That's right. You mind moving your car? You're in my place."

"Mr. Scalisi would like to speak with you. If it's convenient. He's waiting in the car." The man was exceedingly, excessively polite.

"Mr. Vincent Scalisi?" Zalman asked with a very bad knot beginning to spread from his stomach up around his heart. Of course this was the Vinnie Scalisi Lila had referred to, the ex-boyfriend, Vinnie "the Disposal" Scalisi, a well-known unpleasant person. *Oh boy,* Zalman thought as he killed the motor and stepped out of the car, *if I'm alive tomorrow I'm going to strangle Phil Hanning.*

The man led the way to the limo and courteously opened the door for Zalman. Inside, huddled in the enormous seat, a slim young man with curly golden hair sat drinking a Tab. "Thank you so much for coming, Mr. Zalman. Sit down, won't you?"

Zalman took the swivel seat facing Scalisi and decided Lila's ex-boyfriend looked like a wild card. The youngster was clad in an expensive velour workout suit and running shoes and looked way too young, too innocent, too naive, to be Vinnie "the Disposal." In fact, he looked more like a cherub than any grown man Zalman had ever seen. "Mr. Scalisi?" Zalman said doubtfully. "Forgive me, but I thought you were an older man."

Scalisi's merry blue eyes danced like dimes in a slot machine, and he screwed his face into a cheerful smile. "That's Dad you're thinking about! I'm Vinnie Scalisi Junior. Here—my card!"

He handed Zalman an Oxford blue card which read "Scalisi Securities. Investments & Sales. Your Portfolio Is Our Portfolio." There was a Coronado address and phone number. Zalman put the card in his pocket and smiled obligingly.

"Is Lila okay?" Vinnie Junior blurted. Now he looked like a petulant cherub, a cherub with a busted bow and arrow. "Did she mention my name?"

Zalman was confused. Maybe he was "Dear Abby" after all. "Uh, just fine . . ." he mumbled.

"She's a very gentle soul," Vinnie Junior said rhapsodically, "and I'm crazy about her. Do you think she'd take me back? She's older than I am," he said conspiratorially. "She thinks we can't get married because of the difference in our ages. I told her that's outmoded thinking.

She has to free herself from the concepts of the past. What does age matter when you've found your soulmate? We're soulmates! *Soulmates!*"

Vinnie Junior's voice rose and Zalman was afraid he was going to burst into tears. "There, there," he said awkwardly, patting Vinnie Junior on the arm. "She's a fine woman. I'm sure she'll see the light."

"I hope so. You've been very kind, Mr. Zalman. But don't bother her, okay? Let's just say Lila's near and dear to the Scalisi family . . ." Vinnie Junior's voice trailed off as he picked at the Velcro snaps on his running shoes.

"Look, Mr. Scalisi," Zalman said carefully, "a man was killed the other night. Lila was doing business with this man, which means she's involved, and I found the body, which means I'm involved. You know how the police react to this sort of thing. Personally, I have no desire to cause anyone trouble, but there are going to be a lot of questions."

"Ah, yes," Vinnie Junior said sadly. "Sticky Al Hix." He shook his fleecy head.

"I know you wouldn't know anything about that," Zalman said hastily, "but could one of your associates have been over-anxious, perhaps? Trying to help you out somehow, without your knowledge, of course . . . ?"

Vinnie Junior regarded Zalman calmly. "I'm sorry Al cashed out," he said, "but I don't know who did it and I don't care. I love Lila. That's all I care about. If it makes her happy to sell her stuff, okay. I think she's making a mistake but women do what they want. As long as she's happy, Mr. Zalman, I'm happy." He gave Zalman a meaningful look, then held out his manicured paw. "It's been so nice meeting you." As if on cue a man in a sharkskin suit opened the limo door, signaling that the interview was at an end.

Curiouser and curiouser, Zalman thought as he watched the big car squeal out of the underground garage. Sighing, he walked back to the Mercedes and put it away. A few minutes later he barged into his office and found Esther's room vacant. "Esther, my love!" he yelled. "Wherefore art thou?"

"Just a minute!" a muffled voice called frantically through the closed doors to his private office.

"Whaddya doing in there, watching the soaps?" Zalman barked as he stuck his head in the door. Esther was struggling with her skirt and Dex, Lucille's bright young assistant, was struggling with something else. "Oh Jesus." Zalman laughed. "Sorry, kiddies." He closed the door, sat down on Esther's desk, and lit a cigar. A few minutes later she came out, patting her hair into place.

"We were just . . ." she began, very flustered.

"No need to explain. Old Uncle Jerry understands the ways of two young kids in love. But can his nibs afford your lavish tastes on what Lucille pays him?"

"I got big plans," Dex said, grinning unabashedly as he came through the door.

"I'm sure you do, my son," Zalman said. "Did Lucille send you over here or is this strictly social?"

Dex jangled a set of keys. "For the DeLorean. Whoever took it hot-wired it."

"Well, since you're here taking advantage of Miss Wong you can do me a favor. I was going to have Esther do it, but you can run me over to

Slim Honniger's. We're going to pick up the DeLorean, then we'll drop it off at Lucille's, then you can run me back here."

Dex brightened and his beady eyes glared cunningly. "I could just drive it back to Lucille's myself," he suggested casually, "and save you the extra trip." His sharp-featured face contorted in a passable imitation of a smile as he smoothed the razor-thin lapels of his brown Italian wool jacket.

"Thanks anyway," Zalman told him. "But as you are probably aware my sister has an hysterical attachment to that damn car and I promised I myself personally would deliver it to her door. C'mon."

Dex shrugged and gave Esther a peck on the cheek. "Maybe we can have dinner when I get back?" he suggested hopefully.

"Maybe . . ." Esther said vacantly as she scrutinized her porcelain features in a mirror.

Dex drove a faded silver-gray BMW two-door. "It's the up-and-coming car," he told Zalman expansively as he shot them through traffic with a flashy, muscular driving style. "This one's third-hand but it's in good shape. Next year I hope to trade up to a used Mercedes."

"Hope you make it," Zalman said with a great effort at sincerity.

"Thanks." Dex flashed his imitation smile again. "I'm going to law school. Y'know, nights at Southwestern. I think it's a good idea. Lotta big managers are lawyers." He shook his blond head and laughed. "It's weird, though. My classes are full of deputy sheriffs bucking to be D.A.'s. They're big into polyester and they carry guns."

"You're describing half of modern America,"

Zalman muttered, staring out the window and praying the ride would end. Career counseling wasn't his line, and he wished he were in his own car and could make a few calls. It was funny how much business you could do just driving around.

Dex continued to chatter away as he barreled the car over Laurel Canyon toward the Valley. He told Zalman about his childhood in Indiana, his college years in New York, his big jump to California, and how he'd met Lucille and wangled a job with her. His life plan included a fabulous career in the record business, marriage to a woman who could help him attain his goals, and a large house in Encino, if not Beverly Hills. Thirty minutes later Dex rammed the BMW to a rocking halt in Slim Honniger's parking lot and looked at Zalman expectantly.

"Hang on here while I get it straightened out with Honniger," Zalman muttered as he climbed from the car. Dex nodded. Zalman headed for the display room, noticing the DeLorean drawn up in front of the two-story plate glass window. As always, the shiny, lethal-looking car was surrounded by a small, admiring crowd. He went inside and climbed the stairs to Slim's mezzanine office.

"Saw you pull in, pard." Slim grinned, meeting him at the door. He was wearing his Beatles button pinned to a black felt cowboy hat. "Got the John D. all ready for you. Hate to lose it, though. You saw the crowd when you came in? Could be a big attraction around here."

"Terrific," Zalman said, anxious to get moving, to get the car back to Lucille, to get back to Marie. "Listen, Slimbo, I gotta go, huh? I got the keys so everything's jake. Real quick, on another front, I met with Lila this morning and she says nothing doing for you and Phil without the front money. Monty she's willing to pay off on account of the guest list. I threatened her with a court order but I think she knows I'm bluffing. You ain't got much of a case, pal. I'm just bringing you up to date."

"No sweat as far as I'm concerned," Slim said, grinning. "Phil and Monty can do what they want. You told me somebody's gonna make good on the DeLorean so I'm covered, right?"

"Right, Slim, great," Zalman muttered. He glanced through Slim's window and saw Dex outside the showroom, stroking the DeLorean's shark nose. The crowd had momentarily drifted away and as Zalman watched, Dex jangled the key ring speculatively, looked around, opened the gull-wing doors, and slipped behind the wheel. Zalman saw him insert the key and hit the starter. An explosion ripped the DeLorean to pieces.

Zalman dove awkwardly for the floor while Slim hit the deck with the professional ease of an old dogface. There was a wrenching crash as one of the gull-wing doors smashed through Slim's office window, then punched through the plasterboard well beyond the desk and disappeared.

"Jesus!" Zalman heard somebody say from far away, then realized he'd said it himself. His ears were ringing and his hands and face were coated with black, oily soot. He carefully raised his head over the sill of the smashed window and stared down into the wrecked showroom. Although the DeLorean had been outside the showroom the force of the explosion had gone into the room through the big plate glass windows and wrecked the cars on display. The DeLorean itself was a twisted heap of smoking metal surrounded by a charred nimbus. Ugly, serpentine tongues of orange flame licked at the remnants of Lucille's beloved car. Zalman thought of Dex and closed his eyes.

"My God!" a man's voice shouted somewhere, while from outside the showroom a woman's voice screamed, "Fire!" While Zalman watched, a man wearing a "Matchstick Slim" jump suit ran into the showroom with a big fire extinguisher, stepped gingerly through the broken window, and began spraying the DeLorean with soapy foam. He was quickly joined by other men, and within seconds they had a brass-nozzled canvas fire hose in action and were dousing the wreck and the battered showroom cars with massive jets of water. Incredibly, no one was hurt but Dex. At least Zalman didn't see any corpses strewn about. Had the explosion occurred two minutes earlier it would have caught the small crowd which had been clustered around the car.

"Gettin' to be sort of like Bayroot around here," a shaky voice said behind Zalman, and he spun to see Slim's ash-white face staring down into the ruin of his establishment. With trembling fingers Slim fished a bent cigarette from his pocket and managed to get it lit.

"You all right?" Zalman rasped, his mouth tasting of soot, plaster dust, and the acrid flavor of fear and shock.

"Seems like," Slim answered slowly. For some reason, perhaps because he'd been standing several feet farther back from the window than Zalman, he hadn't been touched by the soot. However, a fine powder of shattered glass had evidently sailed over Zalman's head and dusted

Slim's cowboy hat and the shoulders of his tomato-red leisure suit like glittery ice. Slim doffed the hat and gently shook the film of glass off the brim.

"Hey, Artie!" Slim suddenly bellowed through the gaping hole where his office window had been, causing Zalman to jump two feet off the floor. "Don't get water inside them Trans Ams, dammit!"

It was clear that the showroom cars were so severely damaged that wet seat covers were the least of the problem, but Zalman did not bother to point this out. Slim planted his hat back on his bald dome and screwed his cigarette in the corner of his mouth. "Jesus, Jerry," he said mildly. "Think that was supposed to be for you?"

Zalman stared blankly at him for a minute, uncomprehending; then his stunned brain clicked slowly into gear. *Of course,* he thought, *the bomb was meant for me, only Dex blundered into the DeLorean first.* "Poor kid," Zalman said, avoiding Slim's eyes. Suddenly, the big life plan Dex had regaled him with earlier seemed poignant rather than boring. There was a faint whine of sirens in the distance. "C'mon," he said shakily. "I want to take a look at this." He turned and stumbled downstairs without another word.

Picking his path carefully over the wet, debris-strewn floor, Zalman made his way out to the DeLorean and glanced at it quickly. Wedged in the twisted metal mass were obscene, gooey chunks of a substance that had once been human flesh, and Zalman knew if he didn't get away fast he was going to be sick. He went past a knot of salesmen and secretaries and walked into one of the wrecked downstairs offices, picked up the phone on a salesman's desk, and dialed Captain Arnold Thrasher's number. Marie's dad wasn't in, but Zalman told the dispatcher that Thrasher was needed pronto and reeled off Slim Honniger's address. "Tell him he'd better get down here," Zalman said in a dull monotone. "Tell him I said so."

Zalman hung up and looked around the demolished showroom. Slim Honniger was leaning against the far wall, surrounded by flunkies who were jabbering away at him with the relief of close-shave survivors. Zalman knew how they felt. Despite Dex, despite the DeLorean, despite the totaled Pontiacs, the death and destruction could have been a lot worse. Slim hadn't been far off earlier. A time difference of a few minutes and there would have been a real terrorist-style massacre. Zalman felt bile rising in his guts.

He walked across the big room to Slim and pushed through the flunkies. "What's going on, Slimbo?" he demanded coldly, watching Slim's face carefully as he spoke. "You're the only one who knew I was coming over. If the kid hadn't been such an eager beaver I'd be smeared all over your showroom. So you tell me?"

The men and women around Slim shuffled their feet nervously and shifted their eyes, wishing to hell they were somewhere else. Outside, the fire department ambulance arrived and a pair of beefy paramedics charged over to the smoking DeLorean. Slim's glazed eyes seemed to have trouble focusing and when he spoke his voice was low-key, even gentle. "Zally, you don't think I—"

Zalman shrugged, suddenly exhausted. "Not up to me, old buddy," he interrupted. "But I got a feeling you'd better start looking for some representation, dig? F. Lee Bailey or Melvin Belli. Somebody heavy in the crime end of the law biz. And by the way, you'd better start remembering real clearly where you were when Sticky Al died 'cause I think Arnie Thrasher's going to ask." Zalman turned and walked away, for once in his life in no mood for wisecracks.

He went outside and stood around in the glaring, gritty sunlight, waiting for Captain Arnold Thrasher to show up. Meanwhile, fire engines, uniformed cops, the bomb squad, and a coroner's station wagon arrived, and a frenzy of official activity went on around him. Zalman took it in with tired eyes, painfully aware that his impending encounter with Thrasher was going to be very difficult, at best. He didn't have too long to agonize. Thrasher's unmarked green Dodge sedan pulled into the lot about fifteen minutes later and the burly captain walked directly over to Zalman.

"You again!" he barked. "What the hell's going on? What happened here?"

Zalman took a deep breath and told Thrasher the story, keeping it short and to the point, leaving nothing out since he'd arrived at Lila Henderson's that afternoon. The only thing he omitted was the fact that Marie had been and was even now at his house.

"Cripes! This stinks," Thrasher muttered when Zalman was done. He glared up at Slim's gigantic clown balloon floating lazily in the smoggy sky. "Where's Honniger? I've known that jerk since we were kids and I always thought he was a bozo."

"Inside," Zalman said.

Thrasher beckoned to a uniformed sergeant

and told him to keep the TV crews out of the showroom, then motioned Zalman to follow him. They found Slim Honniger sitting disconsolately on a desk, swinging his long legs.

"Hi, Arnie," Slim said dully. "Big damn mess outside, huh?"

Thrasher planted himself in front of Slim and shifted his gut over his belt. "Not as big as the mess you got inside, Slim." He jerked a sausage-sized thumb at Zalman. "He says you're the only one knew he was gonna drive the car, right?"

"I don't know," Slim said. "But—"

Thrasher cut him off. "I didn't like you when we were kids, Slim, and I don't like you now. You used to be a punk car thief and now you think you're some kind of movie star, wearing those stupid clown costumes and cowboy junk. I think maybe you oughta come with me and answer some questions, huh? And when I get through with you I'll feed you to the boys from the Bomb Squad, not to mention Alcohol, Tobacco, and Firearms. Don't worry, you can call a lawyer, since I gather Mr. Always On the Spot Zalman isn't representing you anymore seeing as how you tried to blow his ass up."

Slim slid off the desk and repositioned his cowboy hat firmly on his head. The Beatles button gave him an absurd look. He faced Thrasher, eye to eye. "Arnie, I didn't like you any in high school either and I don't like you now, but I'm going to tell you one little thing. I didn't torch off the DeLorean. Christ, man! Cars are my life! You think I'd wreck a goddamn genuine honest-to-God DeLorean? It'd be like flushing after-tax dollars down the goddamn toilet."

Thrasher shook his big head, disgusted. "You're full of crap, Honniger."

"Generally I am," Slim replied with aristocratic dignity. "But I'm no killer. And as for a lawyer, you bet your ass I want one. I didn't do anything and if you try to say different I'll make life real difficult for you. I'm no hot-wire artist anymore, Arnie. And you're no patrolman. And that means you can't just throw me over the hood of a car and put a bullet through my lungs. Life's a little more complicated these days—"

"If you gentlemen are finished with me," Zalman broke in, "I think I'll be going."

Thrasher turned and faced Zalman. "I'm goddamn not finished with you, Zalman! Not by a long shot! You can go for now but I'll be around to see you later, after I get done with Bozo the Clown here. So be available!"

"I'll count the minutes," Zalman muttered.

Thrasher's face was a red mask of anger. "You're supposed to be a big shot," he said in a tight, barely controlled voice. "You think guys like me are a dime a dozen because you're wearing a two-hundred-dollar tie and I think Sears is a step up. But I protected that girl, Mr. Bigtime. Protected! But first time with you what does she see? A goddamn dead scumbag, for Christ's sake! Stay away from her! You listening?"

"I told you before not to threaten me, Arnie," Zalman said quietly, then turned away and jingled his Gucci key ring in his pocket. He whistled tunelessly under his breath. He didn't want to push Thrasher over the edge.

"You come with me," Thrasher said, stabbing a fat finger at Slim Honniger. He grinned savagely, grabbed Honniger, and roughly propelled him toward the door. Just before they reached it

Thrasher turned and looked back at Zalman, shook his head, and left.

Zalman sighed, sat down at the desk, and dialed Lucille. "I got bad news and I got worse," he told her grimly. "Which do you want first?"

"What is it?" she demanded. "You sound funny. You okay?"

"The DeLorean was blown up and I'm afraid Dex was killed," he said flatly.

"Blown up!" she said in astonishment.

"Just like on 'Cagney and Lacey.'"

"Jesus! What happened?"

Zalman told her what happened, and when he was done Lucille was uncharacteristically silent. "My God," she said finally, her voice oddly calm. "This is connected to Phil and that damned auction, of course."

For once in his life Zalman found himself standing up for his schmuck brother-in-law. "It wasn't his fault, Lucille. Christ, he's gonna feel lousy enough about this without you getting tough on him. He got in over his head, sure, but he didn't know a maniac was mixed up in the thing. It could have happened to anybody."

"Not to you," Lucille told her brother. "Where are you now?"

"Slim Honniger's lot."

"Be there in thirty minutes," Lucille said and hung up. Zalman smiled. Loyalty was the A-number-one rule between Lucille and him. It always had been, it always would be.

Lucille showed up inside the promised thirty minutes, driving Bland's gigantic red Rolls-Royce. Actually, she wasn't driving it as much as aiming it. She embraced him when he got in the car, then glanced at the crowd around the showroom and winced. "Poor kid," she said hollowly. "Listen, what about the . . . ?"

"Coroner's office will take away the remains, for now," Zalman said, sinking back into the cushioned seat, letting a cold jet of air conditioning blow on his sooty, sweaty face. "He got parents?"

"Even *we* had parents, Jerry," she said, pointing the car back onto Van Nuys Boulevard. "I'll take care of it: calling his folks, the funeral, and everything. C'mon, let's go back to the house. You look like you need a drink."

Zalman hunched down in the passenger's seat and remained silent as Lucille wrestled the Rolls through late-afternoon traffic. He was grateful and relieved she'd taken the ugly death of her young assistant and the loss of her beloved DeLorean like the tough guy she pretended to be. It made it easier since he was too numb at this point to offer much sympathy.

He felt terribly sorry for Dex, but as he watched the traffic ooze by, the situation grew sharper in his mind. Someone had tried to blow him up; had wrecked his house, Marie's house, and her office; had killed Sticky Al Hix and now Dex. All of which added up to the inescapable conclusion that the killer was cold-bloodedly vicious and cold-bloodedly cunning. But why? What had he, Zalman, done that was so threatening to someone that they'd want to kill him? He'd blundered onto Sticky Al's murder, but so what? He knew absolutely nothing about it, despite his question-asking of the last several days.

"Zally," Lucille said softly, glancing at her brother, "talk to me. You know it always helps."

"This is real bad, Luce. I don't think I have to

tell you the whole family's on the line 'cause when Arnie Thrasher gets through with Slim and a party named Lila Henderson, which Slim will undoubtedly tell him about, he's going to be back around to see us. And we'd better be prepared with some snappy answers 'cause at this point Phil and I are directly tied to two killings and you can imagine what the cops are going to make of that." He passed a hand heavily over his face.

Lucille blasted the horn at the car she was tailgating, then turned into her street. "Phil's a baby," she said. "He believes in the pot of gold at the end of the rainbow, silly guy." She swung the Rolls into the circular driveway and they saw that both the garage and front doors were wide open. "Look at that!" she snarled. "See what I'm up against? My car is blown up, my assistant killed, and my husband leaves the goddamn doors open just in case the mad bomber wants to drop by and slaughter my entire family." She jerked the car to a shuddering halt, slammed out, and hustled across the driveway to stand in front of the open garage. "Phil! I'm home!" she bellowed. Zalman smiled to himself as he dug himself out of the car. Lucille was in a definite terror mood.

Hanning nervously poked his handsome blond head around the doorjamb leading to the pantry. "Oh hi, honey," he said in an unconscious imitation of Ozzie Nelson. "Everything okay?"

Zalman winced. Even though Lucille had obviously not told her husband about Dex's demise, it was not exactly le mot juste. "Phil," he interjected before Lucille could tool up on her hapless husband, "could I see you for a minute? We'll use your office, Luce," he informed his fuming sister as he maneuvered Hanning through the sliding glass door and out onto the patio.

The Hannings' back yard was filled with the sound of laughter. A small regiment of kids was horsing around in the pool, their shrieks and squeals filling the soft evening air with the easy simplicity of play. The Hanning progeny —Adam, Joshua, and Jennifer—plus a band of neighbor kids were conducting a water polo match against a team which consisted of a frenzied Bland and Biff, Lucille's lone remaining gofer. The two men were thrashing about wildly in the shallow end of the pool in an effort to keep up with the hysterical kids who were climbing all over them. Zalman paused a moment to watch, envying the players their innocence, their ignorance of recent events.

"Mr. Zalman," Bland called, "can I talk to you for a . . . *glurple glurple glurple* . . . " Bland was set upon and ducked repeatedly by the kids. "Time out, time . . . *glurple glurple* . . . king's X, you guys . . ." The kids let go of him and he climbed out of the pool, hitching up his jams around his waist.

"Lucille!" Phil called. "Lucille . . . come on out and watch the kids, will ya! Back in a sec, Zally," he said conscientiously. "We need another grown-up out here." Hanning walked back into the house.

Bland grinned engagingly at Zalman. Considering he was one of the biggest rock stars in the known world, Bland was a remarkably nice fellow. He was a tall, skinny kid with jug ears and a blank stare caused by extreme nearsightedness rather than the vicious cruelty imagined by his pubescent fans. He was kind to his mother and his dog, both of whom were bitches. He signed autographs willingly, still somehow incredulous that an illiterate guy from East London would have the luck to end up in the cushy comfort of glamourland. "It's about me sister, Mr. Zalman," he said politely. "Our Lucille said you could 'elp me wif 'er. Wants to come over. Be a citizen and all. Start 'er own band and contribute to the economy and all. Like that." Bland's thin arms shivered in the cooling air.

"Sure, Bland," Zalman said tiredly. "Shouldn't be a problem. Let's talk about it next week, though, if you don't mind. I've got a lot on my plate right now." He felt the energy dripping out of him like syrup from a tree.

"Righty-o, Mr. Zalman. Any time you say. Thanks a lot, mate, no lie." Bland pumped Zalman's hand enthusiastically and cannonballed back into the pool, sending up a tsunami of major proportions over the patio furniture.

Hanning reappeared through the sliding glass door, Lucille fuming at his heels like a microvolcano.

She opened her mouth to speak and Zalman held up the hand of placation. "Not now, Lucille," he said. "Later, perhaps. But definitely not now. Come with me, Phil."

Zalman and Hanning went into Lucille's home office, a former pool house now filled with a desk, phones, filing cabinets, a couch, and many cardboard boxes containing records, tapes, and yet more files. One wall was taken up with state-of-the-art stereo equipment and another wall was plastered with photographs of Lucille with various industry heavies, some award plaques, and framed gold records. Zalman sank into Lucille's big upholstered desk chair. "Phil," he said, "would you ask Sheri to bring me a large cup of bouillon and a bottle of vodka, please."

Hanning pushed an intercom button and relayed the message to the kitchen, then sat down on the couch. He was wearing white shorts and a lavender cotton T-shirt reading "Be Bland, Be Boring, Be Available." He looked like a gentleman of leisure. "What happened, Zally?" he asked, indicating Zalman's sooty, disheveled appearance, but Zalman just shook his head and refused to speak until Sheri, the Hannings' current au pair-cum-Valley girl padded in and deposited a Thermos of steaming bouillon and a bottle of vodka on the desk.

"Like you guys want anything else?" she singsonged. "I'm like just about to do dinner, you know."

"Not now," Zalman said. "Thanks."

"That's like totally everything that's happening," she said as she left the room.

Zalman fixed himself a Bullshot, took a long drink, then looked directly at Hanning. "This is getting serious, Phil," he said. "Actually, we both knew it was serious all along, but now it's getting close to home . . . your home, I might point out. Dex was killed this afternoon. He got in the DeLorean at Honniger's and it exploded. A bomb, meant for me." Zalman watched Hanning's face closely and saw a look of blank, uncomprehending horror pass over the usually vapid features. If his brother-in-law knew anything about the bomb he was giving an Academy Award performance.

"Oh no," Hanning whispered. "Oh Jesus, poor Dex . . . Oh man, Zally, I'm so sorry."

"We all are, Phil. But now you gotta listen to me. When I saw these gooey chunks of him lying all over Slim Honniger's showroom, well, I'll tell you the truth . . . better him than me. That's what went through my mind. Better him than any of us. That's how we gotta look at it, Phil. I hope you're following me 'cause we'd better do all we can to save our necks."

Hanning put his face in his hands and rested his elbows on his long, bronzed legs. "I'm following you, Zally," he said flatly.

"Who'd want to kill me, Phil, and why? I mean, what am I doing that's so dangerous somebody wants to kill me? You got any ideas, Phil?"

Hanning took his hands away from his face and gave Zalman a level stare. When he spoke his deep, rich voice was uncertain. "Zally, you don't think I had anything to do with the killings? I wouldn't do anything to hurt you. You're part of Lucille, part of my family . . ."

The clink of solid honesty in Hanning's voice rang like a gold coin and Zalman felt ashamed that he'd wondered if Hanning had been involved. "I know that, Phil," he said. "But try and help me out here, will you? Sometimes you . . . let's say, keep things back from me. But if you know anything, and I mean anything, now's the time to come across."

Hanning shook his head. "It doesn't add up, Zally. I know I'm not so bright, but if somebody took the money from Al, why trash your place? Why blow up the car?"

"Either somebody didn't get the money," Zalman said slowly, "or it wasn't the money they were after. Maybe they wanted something else

Al had and took the money to make it look like robbery? So somebody starts following people around in case they've got the money or whatever else? I don't like this, Phil. You could be next, Lucille or the kids. Plus, Thrasher's on our ass again. Once he finishes sweating Slim Honniger and Lila he'll get back to us."

"I don't think he likes me," Hanning said in a puzzled tone.

Zalman laughed harshly. "Just figured that out, did you? Listen, while I think of it, I talked to Lila today." Zalman told Hanning about Lila's offer to pay off Count Monty but her unwillingness to do anything for Hanning and Matchstick Slim. Zalman told how he'd threatened her with a court order but didn't know if she'd believed him or not.

"Ah Christ, Zally," Hanning said wearily. "I'm not gonna worry about it now. I was pissed the other day when I said I couldn't afford to burn off the money. That little twerp Chuck Downley really got to me. It was the way he told me Lila was cutting us guys out. But I mean, look around. We're not exactly on skid row," he muttered with uncustomary pragmatism. "Let's just say it's another screw-up on the part of yours truly and let it go. I'm more worried about all our safety right now than a few thousand bucks, much as I'd like to get it back. Hey, Zally, maybe I oughta get a dog from McCoy? Huh? Like a vicious attack dog?"

"Oh Jesus!" Zalman said out loud. "I gotta call home."

Unexpectedly, Hanning broke into laughter. "You must be in love," he said slyly. "You're beginning to sound like a married man."

"Shut up," Zalman said affectionately. "Sentimentality will take us only so far. Actually, you're getting off very easy. When I came in here my intention was to lean on you hard." As he spoke he picked up one of the phones and punched his home number.

Marie answered on the second ring. "Where are you?" she demanded plaintively.

For a moment Zalman didn't want to tell her about his explosive brush with death but decided that was foolish and wrong since the event directly concerned her. He gave her a brief rundown on the incident at Slim's car lot.

"At least you're all right," she said tightly when he'd finished. "God, I know that sounds stupid. I'm just so glad you're not . . ."

"Me too, kid," he said. "Maybe we'll go back to McCoy's place when I get back. I think we'd both feel a lot safer with him around. Why don't you call him and say we'll come out?"

"Good idea." Her voice was tense with anxiety.

"You got Rutherford there with you?"

"Yeah, right here. He's my big baby."

"Well, anyone comes around, have him bite them. Keep the door locked, hold tight, and I'll be there soon." Zalman hung up, went into the half-bath adjoining Lucille's office, and scrubbed his hands and sooty face. The two Bullshots he'd put away were doing their work, pumping life and vitality back into his bloodstream. "I'm going home," he announced. "I've got a very beautiful girl waiting for me, so what am I doing here with you? Get the keys to the Volvo for me, will you, Phil?"

"Sure, Zally," Hanning said with a smile, glad

to be off the hook even if it was only temporary. "When do you want to leave?"

"About twenty minutes ago," Zalman said.

He could tell she was looking forward to seeing him. She had the brisk scent of perfume just applied and the look of makeup retouched. Even the collar of the shirt she wore—one of his blue shirts—had been turned up so it framed her face with a jaunty air. Rutherford, panting happily past his pink tongue, was at her heels when she opened the front door.

"Hello, sailor," she said joyfully. "Thank God you're safe."

"Down, Rinty," he ordered as Rutherford started to jump on him. He took her in his arms and held her close, pressing the length of her little body against him. "When this craziness is over," he murmured, nuzzling her neck, "want to go to Hawaii or something?"

"Yeah," she said between kisses, "or something. Oh, Jerry, after you phoned I realized if anything had happened I'd really miss you." She squeezed him with surprising strength. "I'm *so* glad you're all right."

"I'd say I'm very all right." He laughed, despite the grim weariness he felt in his bones. "In fact, we'd better cut this out or you'll have to go to bed without your dinner."

She giggled and broke free of his embrace. "I give, I give. Let's go eat and then . . ."

"If I weren't so hungry you wouldn't have to wait for the 'and then,'" he said with a mock leer. He went into his dressing room to change clothes. "Bring your things," he called. "We'll go for Chinese. Then we'll buzz out to McCoy's compound."

"Sounds good," she answered. "He's expecting us. But we'll have to come back here to pick up Ruthiepoo. He's my little sweetie."

"Jesus," Zalman muttered. "It's really gonna be 'Ruthiepoo,' huh? Okay, doll, anything you want. Ah Fong's is close enough. Maybe we can pick up some sweet-and-sour kibble for the pooch."

"Where's the Mercedes?" she asked a few minutes later when she saw the Volvo wagon in the driveway. "Don't tell me that got blown up too?"

"No." He laughed grimly. "I borrowed this from the Hannings. My car's still at the office." He held the door for her and she slipped into the passenger's seat. They sat quietly in the strange car for a moment, admiring the pale purple night sky through the open sun roof.

After a bit she took his hand and squeezed it. "Oh, it's terrible, terrible, terrible about this poor kid who got killed," she said flatly. "I'm not talking about it because I'm trying not to think about what almost happened to you. But I can't help it. What are we going to do, Jerry? We can't hide the rest of our lives. What's going on?"

He didn't know what he was going to say, but the sudden expression of shock and fear sweeping her face stopped him cold. A sharp pain smashed the side of his head and he half heard her cry out as he slumped forward in the seat and his forehead connected with the sharp ridge of the steering wheel. The dashboard blurred out in front of him and he fought a quick but losing battle with unconsciousness . . .

The steering wheel was still cutting into his forehead when he came to. He managed to sit upright, then groaned and gripped his head,

which was filled with sloshing, throbbing pain.
His fingers came away smeared with sticky co-
agulated blood, the side of his head was stab-
bingly painful, and he knew he'd been sapped.
He squeezed his eyes closed until the worst of
the swimming pain passed, leaving the throbbing ache beneath it still hard at work. Slowly,
he opened his eyes again, brought his arm up to
his face, and managed to read his wristwatch. It
was eight o'clock. He'd been out almost forty-
five minutes.

He spun his head toward the passenger's seat,
then groaned as the too-quick movement
brought the sloshing pain back. Of course,
Marie was gone, and in her wake the passenger
door stood open in the darkness. Zalman opened
his own door, carefully got out, and managed to
stay upright only by bracing himself on the side
of the car. "Goddamn!" he said savagely. He
started down the walkway to his front door and
eventually got there.

He fumbled with the light switch, went into
the bathroom, and leaned against the sink. A
thin trickle of blood the color of ketchup began
in his fifty-dollar haircut and ran down his
cheek and neck, and there were silver-dollar-
size circles of shock under his dilated eyes. He
looked like bloody hell and felt like it too. He
soaked a washcloth in warm water and gently
washed some of the blood away, then switched
to cold water and laid a compress briefly against
his head. Since he didn't pass out from excruci-
ating pain he decided he was going to live after
all. He shuffled into the living room, ignoring
Rutherford, who was dogging his footsteps and
whimpering like a coward, then sank down in an

armchair next to the phone. He was about to call Thrasher when the phone rang loudly, startling him and sending stabbing pain shooting through his head again. He groaned, then picked up the receiver and said nothing.

"Mr. Z.?" a tearful voice asked. "Is that you?"

"Esther, how are you, dear?" he croaked, realizing he'd forgotten to call her earlier about Dex.

"Okay, okay." She sighed heavily through audible sniffles. "Lucille told me about Dex and I feel pretty weird about it. I wasn't really that tight with him but it's still weird. Especially since, well, you know, this afternoon and all."

"It's rough, dear," Zalman told her briskly, remembering how he'd blundered in on Esther and young Dex disporting themselves in his office that afternoon. He wanted to sympathize with her but right now he had more crucial things on his mind, like Marie and the fact she'd been kidnapped, like the need to get hold of Thrasher pronto.

"Well," Esther said with another sniffle, realizing the conversation was going nowhere. "I just wanted to see if you're okay." She sounded miffed that Zalman hadn't offered to hold her hand, but he didn't have time for that now. He'd deal with her later.

"Thanks for calling, dear," he said in the same brisk tone. "Try and take it easy." He hung up quickly and was about to dial Thrasher when the phone rang a second time, sending more shooting pains through his head. "Jesus," he muttered and answered it.

"Jerry? It's Isobel. Look, I've got to talk to you. The Undie World thing caved, I mean, it turned out to be a real horror show what with them wanting points up front and all sorts of guarantees that were truly from beyond the limits of our particular galaxy—"

"Isobel," Zalman moaned, "I can't talk—"

"But look, the reason I'm calling is I think I'm onto something big and I want you to look over the papers for me, okay? This new client I picked up, well, he's Duane McMasters, the guy with the LiteBake Tanning Salons? Okay, let's face it, he's the absolute king of tanning and he's got L.A. locked up until the next century, but it turns out he's thinking franchise. I told him that it sounded like LiteBake was certainly the kind of proposition I could get serious about but I wouldn't want to set pen to paper without my attorney giving the paperwork a long, hard look—"

"Look, Isobel, I—"

"So here's the deal. I've got a guy booked for tomorrow morning, then I've got my financial goals class downtown, but on the way back I could swing by your place and look, I *know* you need work, Jerry. I haven't forgotten you, I just want you to know that. I can give you an hour or two and leave the papers for you. Okay? Sound good? Great. 'Bye for now." She hung up.

Zalman stared blankly at the phone and gently set it down. "It's a wacky world," he said to himself. "Truly a wacky world." The phone rang a third time.

There was a brief, confused silence on the other end and then someone said, "I've got the girl." The voice sounded like a bad imitation of Marlon Brando in *The Godfather*.

"Yes?" Zalman said brightly, instantly all

business despite the fact his head was killing him and his stomach felt like it was full of weasels.

"I've got her," the voice said again around the orange slices in its mouth. "And I'll kill her if you don't stay out of my way."

"And you'll let her go if I do everything you want, right?" Zalman prompted.

"Uh, yeah, sure," the voice said, a little confused.

"Put her on so I know she's okay," Zalman commanded.

The receiver on the other end clattered to the floor and the kidnapper yelped as if it had landed on his foot. Zalman listened intently. He could hear the sound of voices rising in argument and despite his fear for Marie, he grinned. She was a feisty little package, no doubt about it.

She came on the line. "Jerry?" she said breathlessly. "Look, I'm okay—" The phone was obviously snatched from her hand.

"Okay, Zalman," the Godfather voice said again, "now you've heard her. If you want to see your little chickapoo again just stay out of my business! Anyway, it'll all be over tomorrow."

"What will be over tomorrow?" Zalman prodded, although he knew full well what the kidnapper meant.

"The auction, dummy! What do you think this is all about, for Christ's sake!"

"Look, bring the girl back," Zalman said, hoping he didn't sound as desperate as he felt. "Take me instead. After all, I'm the guy causing all the problems, right?"

"This isn't a negotiation!" the kidnapper shouted. "I'm in charge here!"

"Right, right," Zalman soothed. "Let me talk to her again, will you? We were interrupted."

There was a brief silence as the kidnapper seemed to consider Zalman's request. Once again, he listened intently, but all he heard was a dull hum in the background, plus the kidnapper's breathing.

"No, I won't," the kidnapper said sulkily. "Just remember what I said. Don't rock the boat!" The line went dead.

Oh boy, Zalman thought, *a crazed killer who does impressions. Thrasher's gonna love this.* This time he managed to get the Van Nuys police station, but the dispatcher said Captain Arnold Thrasher had gone home for the night. Zalman left word where he could be reached and warned the dispatcher if he valued his life and his job he'd better get hold of Thrasher as quickly as modern technology permitted.

When he hung up, his head hurt worse than ever and he felt drowsy. He knew enough about concussions to know he was about to get very sleepy but that whatever he did he mustn't sleep. He stumbled into the kitchen, brewed a pot of strong coffee and washed down two Tylenols with some of it, then poured another cup and started pacing up and down the living room. He drank the second cup and kept shuffling, hoping to walk off the sleep tugging at his eyelids with little lead weights. Finally he sank into an arm-chair, exhausted but curiously no longer sleepy.

A thousand disjointed thoughts tumbled around his bruised brain. Why didn't Thrasher phone? Who had Marie and was she all right? He wished to God crime were as simple as a

Sherlock Holmes movie in which the criminal left a note telling Holmes what to do if he wanted Watson back or the kidnap victim cleverly managed to scatter a trail of luminous paint leading Holmes to Moriarty's lair. But real crime wasn't like that. It wasn't simple and neat. It wasn't a clever puzzle. It wasn't cozy. Real crime was unexpected danger that lunged out of the darkness, that hurt and terrified, that stole someone you loved . . .

Rutherford, who'd been sleeping on the couch, came over, licked Zalman's hand sympathetically, and regarded him with great liquid eyes. Zalman sighed, rumpled the dog's pointy ears, and waited for Thrasher's call.

Once again Captain Arnold Thrasher was displeased. In fact, he seemed so close to inflicting grievous bodily injury that Zalman did his utmost to remain calm and polite when Thrasher reached his house, about twenty-five minutes after the big cop finally returned his call. Carefully, Zalman ran over the story of Marie's kidnapping while Thrasher prowled the length of the living room like a caged bear. When Zalman was done Thrasher threw himself into a Victorian armchair which groaned under his weight and stared at Zalman with barely suppressed malevolence.

"Okay," Thrasher said. "Number one, I'm in charge. Which means I'm calling all the shots. Number two, forget about bringing in the LAPD or FBI 'cause there isn't time for them to do anything. I know, I'm a cop, I'm not supposed to say things like that, but that's how it is. Three, I don't give a lot of weight to this guy's promise to turn her loose tomorrow after the auction. This bozo's already killed twice. Marie can identify him, so he has nothing to lose and a hell of a lot to gain by killing her too. All this adds up to one thing: this guy's gonna be at the auction and we're gonna have to spot him and get him before he hurts Marie. As much as the idea makes me vomit, I need you. You've been nibbling around the edges of this thing for a couple of days and you've already talked to this character. I don't see any other way to play it. You got a drink around here?"

Zalman gestured toward the bar and Thrasher loped across the room, poured himself a triple shot of Black Label over two inches of ice, tossed it down like water, and poured the same again. He stood in the center of the room, swirling his drink and glaring at Zalman.

"Now you tell me Marie's house was wrecked," Thrasher said, puzzled. "Could you explain why in the name of all that's holy she didn't call me two nights ago?"

Zalman stared blankly at the cop. "She's afraid of you, Arnie."

"Afraid of me!" Thrasher exploded. "That's impossible! She's my daughter. I love her."

Zalman shrugged. "Look, Arnie, you're a very scary guy. Hell, I'm an attorney, I get paid to deal with scary types, and even *I'm* afraid of you. C'mon, you can talk to me straight. You're a cop and you're also a big guy and you try to scare people 'cause it makes your job that much easier if they're afraid of you. Am I right or am I right?"

Suddenly, Thrasher's face sagged and he looked like a crestfallen basset hound. "Well," he mumbled, "yeah, okay. But not Marie! She's my little baby! You want a slug o' the mug?" he asked, holding up the rapidly dying fifth of Black Label.

Zalman waved the bottle of scotch away, forced himself to his feet, and stumbled across the room to the bar. "Look," he told Thrasher as he prepared a Bullshot, "you can't turn it off just because you sign out. Of course she didn't want to call you the other night. She *had* to call you when we found Sticky Al, but she sure as hell didn't want to phone you two nights running." A minute later, carrying his drink in one hand and an ice cube in a napkin in the other, Zalman shuffled back to his chair and sank into it. He held the ice cube to his bruised head. "Jesus, this hurts like hell, I'll tell you," he muttered.

Thrasher lumbered over to Zalman. "If she's hurt, if my little baby's hurt, I'll kill you," he said simply. "I'll haul your ass out in the desert and drop you down a well."

"Back off!" Zalman shouted, suddenly tired of Thrasher's bullying. "I want her back too! I think I love her."

"You think!" Thrasher demanded. "What's to think about? Either you love her or you don't. There's no thinking about love with a girl like that. Jeez, you modern guys give me a pain."

"Okay, okay, I love her, dammit," Zalman admitted. "Even though she's too short."

"What are you? The Jolly Green Giant? Just what I need. A half-pint lawyer for a son-in-law."

"Wait a minute here," Zalman backpedaled. "I said I love her. I'm not ready to propose. Besides, Arnie, these days a guy proposes to the girl, not her father. That went out a couple centuries ago."

"Don't call me Arnie," Thrasher said mildly,

mixing himself another drink. "But you'll propose all right. Marie sorta brings out the marriage in a guy. She'll bring a lotta crap in here, I'm warning you." He swigged his drink and stared blearily around the wrecked room. "You oughta get a cleaning lady, you know that?"

"Arnie," Zalman said, realizing he was getting a little drunk himself. "You're missing the point here, aren't you? Marie's been kidnapped by a lunatic killer. I can't ask her to marry me unless we find her."

"See! See!" Thrasher declaimed drunkenly. "You do want to marry her!"

"Jesus," Zalman moaned, shutting his eyes. He felt like he was trapped in a house of mirrors. There was a sudden pounding at the front door, to which Rutherford responded with a small burp. The highly trained guard dog then rested his head between his paws.

"It's McCoy!" a voice called. "Let me in, goddammit!"

Zalman shuffled over to the door and let McCoy in. "Dean," he said brightly. "Look who's here."

McCoy's big face spread open in a Mount Rushmore grin. "Arnie! You again? What damn luck! Boy, I tell you, Jerry, we must be two lucky fellas to see Arnie again so soon. Kicked anybody in the crotch lately, Arnie?"

"I'm going to kill you, McCoy," Thrasher said. "I'm going to rip your ugly head off your body like I shoulda done a long time ago."

"Boys, boys!" Zalman said hastily. "This is no time for fond memories, okay? Let's drop the hostilities. Marie's been kidnapped, Dean. I'm going to need your help." Rutherford, who hadn't bothered to get up for McCoy, whined piteously at the mention of Marie's name.

"Oh boy," McCoy said curtly. "When you guys didn't show up like you said I got worried and drove down. When'd it happen?"

"About an hour and a half ago. I'm not exactly sure."

"Hah!" Thrasher snorted, moodily swirling his drink.

"Arnie," Zalman said, "you've got to cut the attitude if you want to get Marie out of this. You can torture me and McCoy later. Right now the only important thing is finding Marie. Am I right or am I right?"

"Okay, okay," Thrasher barked, and Zalman saw that Thrasher was losing control. In his own morose way the big cop was verging on hysteria. He'd lost the ability to think like a cop.

"Look, we can't do anything more tonight," Zalman continued. "In the morning I suggest you get some of your buddies . . . I know, you said no cops but we're going to need some more help . . . get them over to Lila's in waiter outfits and jogging clothes and we'll try and flush this guy before he loses all his marbles. I'll be there. McCoy'll be there, right, Dean?"

"Right, Jerry. That Marie's a nice girl, Arnie. How'd a creep like you ever get such a nice girl for a daughter?"

Thrasher glowered at McCoy and swigged his drink. He seemed about to respond when he suddenly made a thick sound like gears grinding and fell over sideways on the floor. Zalman and McCoy looked at him, then each other, then Zalman got blankets out of the hall closet and draped one over the big cop's mountainous form.

"I'm living in a world of total loonies," Zalman muttered, heading for his bedroom as McCoy settled down for the night on the couch.

"Yup," McCoy said, arranging his own blanket. "We all are. Nighty-night now."

Zalman crawled out of bed at seven the next morning after sleeping badly, padded into the bathroom, and gently probed his injured head. Despite a dull throbbing in the temporal regions he had to admit he didn't feel too wrecked, no worse in fact than if he were suffering a medium-grade hangover. Gratified to discover he was still alive, he opened the door to the living room and checked on his guests. Thrasher was still asleep, although sometime during the night he'd managed to crawl into one of the Victorian armchairs. McCoy was still on the couch, gurgling softly into his blanket like a sleeping babe. Rutherford had remained on the Persian rug, head on paws. Zalman closed the door, went back to the bathroom, and crawled under a steaming shower, gingerly protecting his bruised places from the strumming water.

As he stood there letting the water pound heat and life back into his body he played and replayed in his mind the frenetic conversation with Marie's kidnapper. In the splash of water on tile memories stirred, but though he concentrated with the intensity of a meditating swami, the truth swirled down the drain with the water.

"Damn," he muttered as he stepped out of the shower and toweled off. A moment later there was a mournful groan from the living room followed by a massive thud as Thrasher evidently fell off the chair with an earth-joggling impact. Zalman winced, hearing his peg-and-groove floor shriek for mercy as the big cop padded heavily across the room.

"Already it starts," Zalman told himself through clenched teeth. A few more moments of peace and quiet and he might have been able to recapture the vague recollections filtering through his brain, but now they were gone. He sighed, shaved, and dressed in chinos, loafers, and a blue linen shirt. With stabbing anxiety he realized the shirt was the twin of the one Marie had appropriated last night and he wondered desperately how she was holding up. Of course, there was always the grim possibility the killer would do something to her before the auction, but that was beyond their frail ability to counteract. They had to keep a positive attitude and hope the guy would trip himself up. Anyway, Zalman told himself as he selected a dark blue summer-weight blazer, it was the only chance they had so they had to play it for all it was worth.

"Coffee?" he asked cheerfully as he went into the dining room.

Thrasher was sitting at the round oak dining table, his obviously throbbing head in his hands. "Please," he gasped without looking up. Zalman brewed a pot so strong it looked like molten lava and carried a cup in to Thrasher, who was now on the phone. He looked a little green but at least he'd managed to make it up on his feet. McCoy was still asleep. Rutherford had taken over Thrasher's spot on the armchair.

"Just do it, Bernie," Thrasher said thickly. "That's right. Ten men. No, you don't get to know what it's about." He covered the mouthpiece and turned to Zalman. "You think these guys oughta wear suits or what?"

"Negative, Bill Blass," Zalman snapped. "Like I told you, jogging clothes, jeans, rock-and-roll T-shirts. Hell, just tell them to wear the same clothes they'd wear if they were working vice in Hollywood."

"Oh," Thrasher said knowingly. "I get it." He growled further instructions into the phone, then hung up. "They'll be there," he said grimly, accepting the cup of coffee.

Zalman felt a sudden pang when he saw Marie's hairbrush, which was still on the dining room table. He thought fleetingly about her auburn hair, wet from the hot tub, then shook his head to banish the recollection. He couldn't afford any distractions. Too much was riding on the next few hours.

A minute later McCoy shuffled past on his way to the kitchen. He poured a mug of coffee, carried it back to the oak table, and slumped into a chair. Rutherford padded around nervously, looking for Marie, his nails clicking on the floor. The three men avoided one another's eyes. No one spoke.

The auction was scheduled to begin at eleven o'clock that morning, and although Zalman got there at ten Lila Henderson's huge house was already a circus. The supposedly unpublicized event had clearly become the worst-kept secret in town. Cars clogged both sides of the street leading to the driveway, and a platoon of green-jacketed parking attendants ran back and forth between them like frenzied worker ants. Zalman abandoned the Volvo to a Pakistani with a laconic grin, intending to leave Rutherford in the car. But as he started to walk away the Doberman leapt out and bounded after him.

164

"C'mon, then." Zalman sighed, in no mood for a contest of wills. He'd known Rutherford only three days but the dog already had him well trained.

The high-pitched snarl that comes only from a large crowd grew as man and dog neared the patio gate, and Zalman stared at Lila's garden in horror. At least three hundred people of all descriptions were packed into the big yard, busily trampling Lila's flower beds and grinding their well-shod tootsies into her lawn. Some people stood in little knots talking while others cruised through the crowd like solitary sharks. Perspiring caterers who'd obviously been overwhelmed by the early crowd struggled to arrange buffet tables and lay out cunningly constructed snacks. A four-piece band had set up at the far end of the flagstone patio and was busy belting out rock-and-roll oldies. But most of the action centered around the long display tables that covered the patio and lawn like stalwart soldiers, holding the items that were shortly to be auctioned off.

Zalman searched the milling crowd and finally spotted Lila near the makeshift podium at one side of the yard, decked out in a flowing lavender chiffon dress that made her look like a predatory butterfly. She was dishing out orders to several muscular young men at the bar while Chuck Downley, wearing a pink dinner jacket, hovered beside her attentively.

"No court order?" Downley inquired apprehensively as Zalman approached.

"Let's just say I have a heart of gold," Zalman said through his phoniest smile.

"Let's just say you were bluffing," Lila countered. "Where's Monty? He'd better be here soon, that's all I can say. People have been showing up since seven this morning! I was still in my nightie when they started invading the place. And yes, we're buddy-buddy. I decided to take him back in 'cause I need him to do the auction. The other two jerks can whistle for it."

She turned impatiently to Downley. "Call Vendome," she snapped, "and have them bring some more scotch, will you?" She was clearly in a state of high agitation. "Here!" she shrieked at a bartender. "What are you doing? If you mix the drinks that strong I'll be broke at the end of the afternoon!"

The bartender wheeled and Zalman saw it was McCoy, looking very unhappy in a tight red mess jacket. "Look, lady," he said unpleasantly, "I've been pouring booze for years. I know my job." He turned back to his thirsty clientele.

Zalman tightened his grip on Rutherford's leash, just in case the Doberman decided to recognize McCoy, but Rutherford was busy stealing a canapé off a table. "See you later," Zalman told the big blonde and, hanging onto Rutherford, he dove into the crowd. He took a fast look around the overstuffed yard, then had a cursory glance at the merchandise on the tables.

"Hello again."

Zalman spun. It was young Vinnie Scalisi, clad in a champagne-colored velour jump suit, his two sharkskin-suited pals at his side. "I saw you talking to Lila," he said shyly. "She say anything about me?"

"She's busy with the auction," Zalman soothed.

"What kind of nut wants Buddy Holly's glasses?" Vinnie Junior asked, gazing at a display table. "Seems kinda like ghoulish to me."

"Everybody collects something," Zalman said brightly, trying to edge Rutherford and himself away.

"Hey!" Vinnie Junior said. "This is kind of neat." He was looking at a stained, collarless jacket once worn, according to a card pinned to the sleeve, by John Lennon in Liverpool. Nearby, a group of well-dressed men were excitedly picking over a stack of black-light posters, and across from them a very young girl with green hair and a nose ring jotted up numbers on a pocket calculator as she cast longing glances at a box of *Yellow Submarine* stationery and a school lunch box featuring the Fab Four. "I might make a bid on this," Vinnie Junior mused, fingering John Lennon's jacket.

"See you later," Zalman said, dragging Rutherford. There was no sign of Marie. What was he going to do? He tied Rutherford loosely to a patio railing and went inside the house. In contrast to the clamor outside, Lila's huge, ugly house was cool and quiet. Quickly and with tremendous attention, Zalman toured every room and looked in every closet. There was no sign of Marie.

He went outside again and stood on the patio watching the still-growing crowd. Nearby, hungry buyers were checking out a large selection of psychedelic posters from the concerts at the Fillmore and twenty or thirty lobby cards for *Help!* and *A Hard Day's Night*. There were several tables devoted exclusively to Elvis, displaying throw pillows, scarves, pajamas, and sneakers. But the obvious pinnacle of Presleyana was an eighteen-inch stand-up Elvis doll made in 1957 by Elvis Presley Enterprises, complete with blue suede shoes and a $2,000 reserve price written on a little card beside it.

Conversations overlapped. ". . . do you see that! 'Chantilly Lace' by the Big Bopper! Yeah, he went down with Buddy Holly. Oh, wow, look, look, look! Remember Woodstock? Yeah, how about Altamont? Oh wow, a Big Brother poster! No, not that Big Brother, stupid! Janis's Big Brother! You're kidding, you mean Ronstadt used to be with a group? McCartney too . . . ?"

Yes, Zalman thought as he watched, the outstanding feature of the gathering was naked, unadorned, uncloaked greed. "I want it! I want it! I gotta have it!" was the leitmotif of the morning as Hollywood's well-heeled guys and gals about town salivated over Lila's nostalgic treasures.

Thrasher appeared through the patio gate and halted stock-still in horror, aghast at the sight of the eccentric crowd. He looked anything but normal himself, attired in a lime-green satin bowling jacket with "Bowling for Life" embroidered in splashy scarlet letters on the back, madras Bermuda shorts, black-and-white tassel loafers, and a pair of yellow-tinted aviator glasses. Actually, Zalman realized, the big cop fit right in. Zalman went over to him.

"Any sign of Marie?" Thrasher asked tightly, continuing to scan the crowd with a practiced eye. Zalman shook his head. "I've been checking out the parking area," Thrasher reported. "Vans, big cars, stuff where you could stash a—" He broke off, momentarily horrified at what he'd been about to say, then shot Zalman a gimlet look. "This place is a goddamn circus!" he snarled.

He was right. The decibel level was approaching heavy-metal intensity as the Henderson auc-

tion took on a manically festive beat. Quite a few
people had taken advantage of the nostalgic air
of the occasion to bedeck themselves in fancy
dress, and along with the comparatively normal
punks, urban cowboys, and lumber jills, Zalman saw belly dancers; Queen Elizabeth I; a
fairy godmother of indeterminate sex sprinkling
glitter on the unwary with a trick wand; a snake
charmer draped with a sleepy, self-satisfied boa;
and a passel of swarthy South Americans who
looked like they'd purchased the pickpocketing
concession.

Suddenly, Count Monty made a sweeping entrance through the patio gate, surrounded by a
flying wedge of courtiers. His immense bulk was
encased in a flowing purple robe embroidered
with silver comets, crescent moons, and radiating stars. He looked like a gargantuan version of
Mickey Mouse as the Sorcerer's Apprentice.

"I dunno what you did, man," he told Zalman
breathlessly as he passed, "but you did good.
Lila's taken me back in. Later." He went on to
the podium, where his flunkies busied themselves adjusting the mikes while Monty and Lila
smothered each other with kisses.

"Another one of your bozo clients?" Thrasher
asked stonily. "What is it with you, Zalman? You
only represent guys that wear weird clothes?
Jeez." The big cop moved off into the crowd.

Zalman saw Lucille, Phil Hanning, and their
kids come in, flanked by Bland, various girlfriends, secretaries, hangers-on, and pals.
Bland and the kids instantly took off for the pool
and dived in with much splashing of water.
Hanning, who looked sick to his stomach, was
wearing a BLAND RIPS IT! T-shirt and had his

CALL JOHN button prominently displayed. Spotting Monty and Lila he made a zigzag run through the crowd to their position by the podium. But despite the shouting that ensued no one paid Hanning any mind, not even Thrasher's athletically clad men who were simultaneously circulating and trying to blend into the foliage.

Zalman continued to study the crowd frantically. He spotted Rutherford at the far end of the pool. The dog had pulled his leash loose and was now sniffing about the shrubbery, evidently preparing to perform a basic canine ritual.

By now the noise level was deafening. Kids were shrieking, avaricious patrons were shouting, music was pounding, and glasses were clinking. "Shit!" Zalman bellowed in frustration. It wasn't often that his height was a handicap, but this was definitely one of those times. He couldn't see anything but a forest of bodies and, abandoning all embarrassment, he grabbed a rickety gilt chair, stood up on it, and looked out over the seething crowd.

Suddenly, a familiar voice rumbled sonorously through the public address system. "Folks! Folks! Your kind attention, please!" Count Monty's deep, thrilling tones undulated over the throng. "If you'd all settle down," Monty boomed, "we'll get this thing under way." He spread his arms in a gesture of benediction as the crowd burst into applause, then grew gradually silent. Monty's presence seemed to quell the feverish anxiety and greedy tension radiating through the air. The noise level fell to zero.

From his vantage point on the gilt chair Zalman saw Rutherford at the far end of the garden suddenly snap to attention like a pure-bred pointer, then emit a hideous howl. Instantly, the Doberman raced for the pool house. At the same moment the heater motor kicked in, its catty, well-oiled purr clearly audible across the length and breadth of the big yard, and Zalman felt like the Red Sea had just parted at the door of his Mercedes.

He recognized the sound: it had been in the background during the kidnapper's phone call. Rutherford was now clawing frantically at the pool-house door, and as the dog whimpered and whined, Zalman, atop his chair, saw something else: Chuck Downley was staring aghast at Rutherford. Suddenly Zalman felt the deep, animal growl of the caveman rise from his throat.

"You!" he screamed at Downley in the momentary silence. He leapt forward, the rickety little chair teetered, and he catapulted into the arms of a very big, very sexy blonde wearing nothing but a skimpy bikini, a Walkman, and roller skates. Cradling him like a baby the astonished skater scissor-kicked backwards as her wheels grappled futilely for traction on the flagstone patio; then both she and Zalman crashed into a table laden with a mound of iced shrimp sculpted into a replica of an electric guitar. Instantly, Zalman wrenched free from the sticky blonde and careened over flagstones slippery with squashed shrimp, inadvertently pushing a fat man in a Panama hat and a gentleman wearing a burnous into the portable bar, which collapsed under their weight, sending bottles and glasses flying. Zalman kept on going.

"Get that sonuvabitch!" he shouted, hoping Thrasher or one of his men would help him out. But since Zalman had momentarily forgotten

Downley's name, Thrasher and his minions
didn't know which sonuvabitch to get and settled for darting back and forth like confused
linebackers. There were angry shouts from
those mired in shrimp and champagne and in-
creasing laughter from the onlookers.

Zalman shoved his way forward through the
crowd like an icebreaker and was rewarded with
a glimpse of Downley in his pink tux dashing for
the pool house. Zalman knew he'd been right!
Marie was inside, no doubt about it. As he
barreled forward an unwary waiter with a tray of
drinks stepped in his way and Zalman unhesi-
tatingly straight-armed the man into the pool,
where he was welcomed with shouts of delight
by Bland and the kids. Dimly, through all the
racket, Zalman heard Hanning calling to him
over the loudspeakers. "Zally, Zally, what's the
matter?" Hanning asked anxiously, his rich actor's voice echoing through the crowded garden.

Zalman ignored him, determined to beat
Downley to the pool house. Now Downley was in
the open, free from the crowd around the podium, and he was picking up speed. He bounded
around the memorabilia-laden tables with the
cornering finesse of a Porsche, reached the far
side of the pool, and then unexpectedly collided
with the fairy godmother, who pitched into the
pool with shrieks and an explosive cloud of
glitter. Arms flailing, Downley followed her into
the water, where the kids swarmed over him
with gleeful shouts.

Gulping air, Zalman finally reached the pool
house, rammed the padlocked latticework door
at a dead run, and smashed it off its hinges. He
staggered inside and saw Marie, gagged and

bound, lying on her side on a green canvas chaise lounge, her wide brown eyes flashing with surprise, hope, and astonishment. "Murgh, murgh!" she huffed through her gag as Zalman blinked whirling little stars out of his eyes and shook off clinging strips of lath. To add to the confusion, Rutherford practically knocked him over in his anxiety to reach Marie, then lay down at her feet and began to lick her toes ecstatically.

A split second later Zalman's head cleared, and he sprang forward to free Marie just as a dripping, sputtering Chuck Downley burst into the room behind him. "You've ruined everything!" Lila's half-brother screamed, pointing a massive 9 mm automatic at Zalman. "I'll kill you! You've wrecked my entire life!"

Zalman bravely stepped in front of Marie and faced the soggy lunatic. "Look, pal," he said, still unable to remember the lunatic's name, "let's try and calm down here. I'm an attorney. Believe me, we can work something out."

"Ha!" Downley snorted derisively, waving the evil-looking 9 mm around like a sultan's scepter. "There's no working *this* out, Mr. Attorney! It's over for you. I can't stand it anymore, you hear me! Lila treats me like shit! Her own flesh and blood! Rich people have *everything!* You think a man my age wants to be a *houseboy!* I see it all but I have nothing! *Me,* with a Ph.D. in history from Berkeley! Who wants history teachers, huh? History's in the toilet! This auction was my last chance to score some big bucks and now you've *ruined it!*"

In his fury Downley jerked the trigger and the gun went off with a horrendous boom, but lucki-

173

ly the round tore harmlessly through the shake roof. "See?" he said in a hushed voice through a crooked grin. "I'm really gonna do it. First you, Mr. Big Shot Attorney, and then the girl. Then my bitch sister. Who says revenge isn't worth it?" He laughed maniacally and took careful aim down the long anodized barrel.

Still shielding Marie, Zalman sighed and closed his eyes. Mother of mercy, he wondered, was this the end of Zalman? Could a spaced-out lunatic of a houseboy with a gun snuff out the entire career of a Bev Hills lawyer with every-thing on the upswing? It didn't seem possible. And where the hell were McCoy and Thrasher and his merry men? They were supposed to take care of this situation. Why did he, Zalman, have to do everything and take all the risks?

"*Farf!*" The gun went off. The explosion was followed by a strangled "Aaargh," the thud of colliding bodies, and various groans. Seeing that he wasn't dead yet Zalman opened his eyes and saw Phil Hanning on the floor in front of him, his right shoulder bleeding heavily, Down-ley's 9 mm gripped like a club in his left hand. Downley was on his knees too, whipping his blond head from side to side, clearly dazed.

Zalman realized what had happened. Recall-ing a piece of business from the single film he'd appeared in years before, Hanning had wrestled the pistol away from Downley and in the process had taken a slug in the shoulder. Hanning had actually performed an identical stunt in the spaghetti Western *Rio Locos,* although then, of course, the bullets had been blanks and the blood marinara sauce. Without hesitation, Zal-man leapt on Downley's back before he had time to recover. At almost the same instant Thrasher came panting through the pool-house door, followed by McCoy and several large cops in jogging clothes.

"Baby!" Thrasher cried. "Daddy's here. Everything's okay!" He completely ignored Zalman's bronc-busting act as he knelt down beside Marie and put his Magnum on the floor.

Marie made muffled sounds through her gag. Rutherford whined like the coward he was. Hanning moaned, tried to get up, then fell over again. And Zalman kept punching Downley on the back of the head while the houseboy yelled, "Will you get off, pleaeeese?"

McCoy grabbed Zalman, the cops grabbed Downley, and Thrasher finally succeeded in gently peeling the gag from his daughter's mouth. "Jerry!" she cried in a strangled voice. "Are you all right?" She struggled against the nylon ropes as Thrasher tried to untie them.

Zalman, a little dizzy, shook his head to clear it. "I think so," he muttered. "I don't seem to be dead. Are you okay?"

"Sore and stiff," she said, managing a smile as Thrasher helped her to her feet. "Hi, Dad," she added as Thrasher enveloped her in a bear hug.

Hanning moaned again, and suddenly Zalman remembered the terrible crash the 9 mm made when it went off. He knelt beside his brother-in-law. "Phil?" he asked gently. Suddenly, Marie was at his side.

"Zally, what happened?" Hanning asked in a thick voice. "I did okay for once, huh? He was gonna kill you, Zally."

"He would have killed me, too, if it hadn't been for you," Zalman said. He lifted the torn edge of Hanning's sleeve and saw that the shoulder looked like raw meat. If the ugly wound had been a couple of inches to the left . . .

"Get an ambulance, dammit!" Zalman ordered, turning to Thrasher. He saw that one of Thrasher's men was already on the pool-house phone summoning help. "You saved my life, Phil," Zalman said softly. "Marie's too."

Hanning smiled back at him like the sun. "You think? That's really great. Nobody's gonna hurt my family if I have anything to say . . ." His voice trailed off as he momentarily blacked out.

"Hurry up with that ambulance!" Zalman shouted.

"It's on the way," Thrasher assured him in an undertone. He took off his green satin bowling jacket and laid it over Hanning. "We gotta keep him warm," the big cop explained tenderly. Another cop doffed his zippered sweatshirt and did the same, and Zalman rolled up his blazer as a pillow. Even Rutherford got into the act, snouting Hanning gently and whining piteously until Marie pulled him back.

Meanwhile, Downley was sobbing hysterically in the background. "Will you shut the hell up?" Zalman told him fiercely. "Can't somebody get this guy out of here? What the hell's your name anyway, buster?" This set Downley off on a fresh torrent of tears as Thrasher's men led him away, past a near head-on with Lucille, who chose that moment to burst into the room.

"Philly!" she cried. "My God, he's bleeding! Jerry, do something, for Christ's sake! You're an attorney!" She knelt beside her fallen husband.

"Help's on the way," Zalman told her, trying to sound like a take-charge guy. "Try and stay calm."

Zalman felt a tug at his elbow and turned to see Marie looking up at him with shining eyes. "You stood in front of me when he had the gun," she whispered, her eyes going soft-focus. "I love you."

"I love you too," he whispered back, patting her little hand.

"I saved 'em," Hanning told his wife proudly as he emerged from his faint. "Tell her, Zally, how I saved you guys."

Suddenly, a little man wearing a wine-colored velour jump suit came into the room, carrying a little black bag. "Let me through, please!" he said crisply. "I'm Dr. Irving Kipness," he announced to no one in particular. "Ah, this is the patient!" He knelt beside Hanning, quickly examined the wound, opened his little bag, took out sterile compresses, and applied them. "A lucky thing my wife always makes me carry my bag in the car," he told Hanning conversationally. "Actually, I'm a dermatologist, but I guess I haven't forgotten my basic medicine." He chattered away as he prepared a syringe and administered an injection. Almost at once the sedative hit Hanning, his head flopped blissfully into Lucille's lap, and he slept like a lamb.

"Will he be all right, Doctor?" Lucille begged. In the distance the wail of sirens could be heard drawing closer.

"Oh yes," Kipness said confidently, closing his bag. "The bullet completely missed the artery and bone. There's muscle damage, of course, but when you think how bad it could have been, well . . ." He shrugged his wine-colored shoulders and looked around the pool house curiously. "By the way," he told Marie, "that's lovely skin you've got, young lady."

"Why, thanks," Marie said, brightening. "I'm very careful never to go out in the sun."

"If only all my patients were so wise." Kipness sighed. "Just keep up your moisturizer and you won't go wrong."

Kipness stepped back as paramedics from the Sherman Oaks Fire Station trotted into the room. He told them what he'd done for Hanning, and they transferred him to their gurney and rolled him away at a run. "Well," Kipness said cheerfully, "back to browsing. Actually, I don't go in for this silly business, but my boy collects Iron Butterfly. He wants to be a songwriter. Medical school isn't good enough for him." He chuckled benevolently and left.

Zalman was suddenly weighted down on one side by Lucille and on the other side by Marie, both women tenaciously latching onto an arm. "There, there, girls," he comforted, maneuvering them toward the smashed door. "Everything's jake, as the girl said to the sailor. Get my coat, will you, Arnie?" he added, catching Thrasher's baffled glance; then, smiling broadly, he led Marie and Lucille out into the sunny morning.

At six o'clock that evening Zalman escorted a radiant Marie Thrasher through a writhing knot of feral entertainment reporters jamming the corridor outside Phil Hanning's luxurious hospital suite and past a rent-a-cop whom Lucille had stationed at the door. McCoy, beer bottle in hand, followed them into the room, although Rutherford, now promoted to hero-dog status, had to remain in the Mercedes.

Inside, Hanning was propped up in bed, wearing a large bandage on his right shoulder and a dreamy smile on his face. Lucille hovered adoringly at his side. The big TV was tuned to "Entertainment Tonight."

Hanning waved weakly at the newcomers with his good hand. "'Actor Foils Killer! Auction Action!'" he quoted blissfully. "Didja see all the reporters outside? I gave a lot of interviews." Despite Hanning's meager acting career Hollywood had evidently decided to reclaim him as one of its own, now that he was front-page news. "Paramount TV called me about a guest spot. And Aaron Spelling called. Aaron Spelling!" Hanning's voice was reverent. "Me! He called me!"

Zalman felt Marie elbow-jab him in the ribs and managed to choke down the wave of manic laughter rising from his guts. "You were terrific, Philly," he said straight-faced.

Marie bent over Hanning's bed and kissed him lightly on the cheek. "Thanks for everything, Phil. Without you, well, I don't like to think about it," she said gratefully, glancing at Zalman.

"It was nothing," Hanning lied modestly. "The guy was nuts. Did you find out what he was after?" he asked Zalman.

"Yes and no," Zalman said. "I talked to Arnie Thrasher a little while ago and he says Downley confessed to everything, right after he got a feeler for the book rights to his story. Like you say, Phil, Downley's a little nuts. At first, he was merely going to hijack the front money from poor old Al and rhumba down to the West Indies. But Al wouldn't give him the dough and Downley, who doesn't like people who say no, freaked out and killed him, then stuffed Al in the fridge, hoping he wouldn't be discovered until after the auction. The really scary part is that Downley was still in Al's office when Marie and I showed up. He was hiding in the shower stall when we discovered the body."

"My God," Marie breathed. "You didn't tell me that!"

"Yeah," Zalman said soberly, "I know." He patted her hand. "Downley was about to search Al's office when we came in, and he heard *us* search the office but couldn't see us or be sure we hadn't found the money or something telling us where it was. That's why he trashed our places looking for it. When I started nosing around, checking up on the partners and Lila, Downley panicked again and blew up the DeLorean, hoping to get me. He was at home when I interviewed Lila and was on an extension phone when I told Slim I'd be around later to get the car. Lila figured I was bluffing about an injunction but Downley wasn't so sure. He'd already killed once. With me out of the way he figured he'd be able to knock over Lila after she got her hands on the auction money. I went out to Thousand Oaks yesterday afternoon to meet McCoy, so Downley had plenty of time to get over to Slim's, find the car out back, and rig it. He used to be an army combat engineer, can you believe it? Knows about plastic explosives and timers and all that 'Mission Impossible' stuff."

"That guy's defending our country!" Lucille moaned. "No wonder . . ."

"So where's the front money?" McCoy asked, belching decorously. "Somebody's got to have it."

180

"I bet Sticky Al hid it really good," Marie chimed in. "I told you he was always hiding things for no reason, like that Beatles pin. By the way, where is it anyway, Jerry? You said I could have it for a souvenir," she wheedled.

"And never let it be said I renege on a promise to a lady." Zalman smiled, withdrawing the pin from his jacket. "Well, rarely anyway."

"Here," Hanning said magnanimously, as if he were parting with the Star of India, "take mine too." He took his CALL JOHN pin out of the nightstand drawer and handed it to Zalman to give to Marie. Hanning's eyes narrowed and took on a slightly cunning look as he regarded his brother-in-law speculatively. "Say, Zally," he said with studied nonchalance. "If I get any work I've been thinking of going in on this singing cowboy museum a friend's starting out in Hemet. He's got their saddles and stuffed horses and old guns and boots and gear. The public'll pay good money to see it, don't you think? All I need is fifty thou to get in as a partner. What do you think, huh, Zally?"

Zalman balanced the two Beatles pins in his hand. "Sounds very interesting, Phil," he soothed. "We'll talk about it next week when you feel better. We've got to go," he announced abruptly, then kissed Lucille on the cheek. "Talk to me later," he called as he hustled Marie and McCoy out the door.

"But, Zally . . . " Hanning called as the heavy door whooshed shut behind them.

"What's the big rush?" Marie asked as Zalman hustled them down the corridor. "After all, he saved our lives. The least we could do is hang out."

"There's plenty of time for gratitude when we clear up a few things," Zalman said absently as they went into the parking lot. McCoy let Rutherford out of the Mercedes and the Doberman immediately visited the Alfa parked next door, left his calling card, and looked very pleased with himself. Zalman was tinkering with the metal backing on Sticky Al's CALL PAUL button.

"What're you doing?" McCoy asked, fishing out another beer from a little Styrofoam cooler in the back seat of the Mercedes.

"Boys and girls," Zalman said, still struggling with the backing, "the deductive brilliance that's made my name a byword in legal circles tells me that Al's pin is considerably heavier than Phil's pin. But I can't get the backing off."

McCoy grunted, tucked his beer bottle under his arm, took the pin from Zalman, and ripped the metal back off with his teeth. Inside the pin, in the curvilinear space between the enamel face and the separate backing, a small brass key was fastened to the enamel with glue. McCoy chipped it loose with a thumbnail and handed it to Zalman. Engraved on the sticky key was the legend "Manny's Meats. #49." There was a Figueroa address.

Downtown Los Angeles was dark and practically deserted when Zalman parked the Mercedes in front of a long, shadowy brick building with a small neon sign proclaiming "Manny's Meats. Cold Storage Lockers." The grimy building was in a neighborhood that looked like it dated from the 1920s. Walls were black with soot; small, evil-looking windows were painted over; and the sidewalk in front was stained with decades of chewing gum, motor oil, and worse.

There were no lights anywhere, no pedestrians, and only a few parked cars.

"I wish we'd waited until morning," Marie said nervously from the back seat as she checked out the street. "It looks like a Diane Arbus photo around here."

"What?" Zalman mocked. "Not interested in the thrill of capture, winning the prize, grabbing the brass ring, et cetera?"

"Sure, sure," she muttered apprehensively, "but in the daylight. This place probably looks half-clean around high noon."

"Don't worry, Marie," McCoy said from the passenger's seat, reaching back and giving Rutherford the last of his bottle of beer. "Anybody messes with you, me and Ruth'll fix them, right, Ruth?" But Rutherford's only comment was a beery burp and McCoy shook his head sadly. Everybody got out and McCoy pounded heavily on a thick, plate-glass front door screened with a filthy venetian blind.

After an interval the blind's louvers parted and a pair of beady eyes peered out. "Whatja want? We're closed up," a reedy voice called through the glass. "Come back tomorrow if ya got business."

Zalman and McCoy smiled happily. "See," Zalman told Marie. "Timing's everything. If we'd waited, odds are your dad would've beaten us to the punch. I know it's late," he called through the door in an authoritative voice, "but I'm an attorney. Here." He shoved his card through the mail slot.

There was a brief silence; then the door opened a smidge on a brass chain and a thin old man with a fringe of ratty hair beneath a bald dome poked his face out and looked them up and down. "Whatja want?" he wheezed. "Who you looking for? I'm Manny and this is my place. Don't want no trouble."

"Can we come in, sir?" Zalman said heartily. "We're going to need your help. An important legal matter . . . large sums . . . untold wealth . . ." He coughed into his hand.

"Didn't think you were looking for me," Manny sniffed, unhooking the chain and letting them in. "Never did have any damn luck with money. Won thirty bucks at Santa Anita, though, right after I got outta the service in '45," he remembered fondly.

He turned his back on them and sat down in a green Naugahyde easy chair in front of a large color TV with the sound off. A TV tray with the remains of Manny's supper was placed next to the chair. The room was a combination office-apartment, not unlike Sticky Al's office, Zalman noted, glancing around at the cramped, minimal setup. There was a heavy insulated tin door on a far wall, evidently leading to the cold storage warehouse.

Zalman took the brass key from his pocket and showed it to Manny. "This from one of your lockers, by any chance?" he asked. He could feel Marie wiggling excitedly next to him. Even the normally sleepy Rutherford seemed churned up, and McCoy nudged him a couple of times with his boot to make him heel.

Manny squinted at the key through watery eyes, said "Humph," and turned back to the silent TV, where Paul Newman as Harper was facing off with Arthur Hill. "Number 49," Manny mumbled as if he'd known it all along. "You're too late if she's the one you're after.

Funniest damn thing," he said, his eyes still on the screen. "Lady come by this morning to get in number 49 but didn't have no key. Said she lost it, so I had to charge her ten bucks to give her the spare. She was kinda irritated but them's my rules. I can't go around giving out keys like they was candy or I'd be outta business in a month. Folks forget the keys all the damn time. Why, you wouldn't believe what—"

"Yes, yes, I'm sure," Zalman broke in politely. "But if you don't mind, sir, back to number 49, the lady—"

"I was getting to it." Manny wheezed irritably. "So she goes in to get some meat, she says, and stays in there a real long time. Then she comes out, gives me a fifty, tells me the meat's mine, I should go ahead and take it. She won't be renting the box no more."

The old man smiled happily. "When I go back to look I find about twenty cases of franks in there, in number 49. Guess I'm lucky some ways after all. Franks're my favorite supper, next to Spam, of course." Manny scraped up a dripping forkful of franks and beans, loaded it into his mouth, and chewed contemplatively.

"Do you know her name, by any chance?" Zalman asked with a sinking feeling in his stomach. "What was her name?"

"Why, Gladys Hix, of course," Manny said grouchily. "You don't think I'd let just any dame —excuse me, miss," he said in an aside to Marie—"any lady go in there, do you? We pride ourselves on our service here. That locker belongs to Mr. Al Hix. Real nice boy, Mr. Hix. He come by about a week ago and give me some money too, twenty bucks it was. When I asked him what for he just said if I didn't see him by today I should call this number." Manny pulled a crumpled piece of notepaper out of his breast pocket and peered at it. "I should call this number and tell Mrs. Hix to open the locker. On account of that I phoned this morning just like he said and she come right down. Say, anything wrong? You folks look like you just lost your best friend."

"No, no," Zalman said, forcing a smile. "Nothing of that sort. You've been most helpful, Mr. . . . ah, Manny. Cleared up many questions . . . most grateful . . . ahem . . ." As he mumbled, Zalman edged Marie, McCoy, and Rutherford toward the door. "Thank you so much."

"You're real welcome, I'm sure," Manny said from his chair. "By the by, that's a real nice little dog you kids got there." McCoy shot Manny an incredulous look as Zalman shooed them out and closed the door with a rattle of louvers.

Outside, it was darker than when they'd arrived at Manny's, although a streetlight had come on, bathing the bleak scene with thin gold light. Zalman felt his shoulders slump. He jingled the keys in his pocket and whistled tunelessly. McCoy leaned on the Mercedes and stared at the toes of his boots. Marie regarded them quizzically. There was a long moment of silence.

"Well, boys and girls," Zalman said with a sigh, "as Justice Holmes used to say, win a few, lose a few." He laughed hollowly, thinking mournfully of the lost thirty grand. How sweet it would have been to have taken the final round.

"I bet Gladys is halfway to Hawaii by now." McCoy chuckled. "Whaddya think Al was up to, anyway, Jerry? Did he steal the front money or was he hiding it until it was the time to pay Lila or what?"

"We'll never know," Zalman said, leaning on the car. "Maybe he had some other promotion going on the side and planned to use the dough for a few days before replacing it. Could have been a rat hole, like Marie said. He was a devious guy, Al, but he had sense enough to cover himself in case anything went wrong."

"Look at it this way," Marie called, rumpling Rutherford's ears while the big black dog greased against her lovingly. "Gladys Hix needs the dough worse than any of us." She shrugged and Rutherford frolicked and whined happily. "Okay, okay." She laughed, petting him again. "At least we have our little woojum-sweetums." She kissed the dog's sleek head.

Zalman and McCoy looked at each other in the murky gloom that suddenly seemed less menacing. McCoy shrugged and looked at Zalman. "Whaddya say, Jerry?" he asked. "Ruth ain't a bad dog. You could get used to him."

"Not in this lifetime I couldn't," Zalman said. "But it's up to you."

"Say there, Marie," McCoy said heartily. "How'd you like to have ol' Ruth here for your very own?"

"You mean it?" She squealed happily. "He's just the cutest little thing. Thanks, McCoy, you're really sweet. Come on, woojie," she said to Rutherford. "Get in the car." Rutherford promptly hopped into the driver's seat of the Mercedes and rested his head on the steering wheel photogenically.

Zalman walked over to the door, bent down

and stared menacingly at the dog. "Back seat, ferret face," he said. Rutherford climbed over the seat and into the back of the car.

"That's great," Zalman muttered. "I got five thousand dollars' worth of leather upholstery here—the dog's gonna rip it to shreds with his toenails. Maybe I should just forget it, run down to Tiajuana and have the thing tuck-and-rolled in vinyl, ground-glass paint job, the whole deal."

Marie was giggling. "What, Jerry honey? You say something?"

"Nothing, nothing . . . McCoy, I'll drop you off at your car."

An hour later, Zalman, Marie and Rutherford pulled up in front of her house in Studio City. Marie opened the front door and let out a squeak of shock. "I forgot it looks so awful in here," she moaned. "This is soooo grim." She'd realized all over again the terrible damage that Chuck Downley had done to her antique-filled house in his futile search for Sticky Al's package.

"Hey hey hey," Zalman said, taking her in his arms. "Don't let it get to you. C'mon, pack a bag, and then you and Rutherford and I'll go over to my place. In the morning I'll get my nutty maid over here and she'll straighten everything out. Might take a while, but I was thinking maybe you and I would run over to Hawaii for a week or so. Relax, soak up some rays . . . How about it, doll?"

Marie nestled deeper in his embrace. "You're a real take-charge guy, aren't you, Jerry?" She smiled up at him. "I like it. It's so old-fashioned it's almost twenty-first century. Okay, let me get a few things together. I'm kind of tired of wearing your clothes . . . I won't be long." She went down the hall and into the bedroom.

Zalman looked over at Rutherford, who was amusing himself by pulling stuffing out of Marie's slashed couch, tossing it in the air and snapping at it.

"God, you're a pathetic imitation of a canine, but it looks like we're gonna have to be palsy-walsys. *Jesus*." Zalman shook his head. "Now *I'm* doing it. C'mon, Ruth, let's you and me go forage." Rutherford leaped up and bounded down the hall to the kitchen, clearly thrilled by the idea of food.

Zalman found a box of Ry-Krisps in the cupboard and tossed one to Rutherford, who leaped up, caught it on the fly, and crunched it merrily, sending a shower of crumbs all over the kitchen floor. "Very good," Zalman told him. "I'm impressed." He tossed another cracker in the air and Rutherford repeated his performance, leaping high to catch it.

"Hey, Marie," Zalman called. "Rutherford knows a Stupid Pet Trick. C'mere and look." He tossed yet another cracker to Rutherford, higher this time, and once again the dog leaped up to catch it. Despite himself, Zalman had a sudden feeling of affection for Rutherford. Okay, so Gladys Hix had found the dough first. Marie was right; Gladys needed the money . . . Zalman felt better than he had in a long time.

"Hey, Marie," he called again, tossing another Ry-Krisp to Rutherford just as Marie stuck her head around the corner.

"What is it?" she said just as Rutherford was arcing into the air. Momentarily distracted, Rutherford collided with the large plastic model of the spaceship Enterprise that hung from the ceiling, sending it crashing into Zalman's face.

"AAARRRGGGHHH!!!" he shrieked.

"Jerry, darling, are you all right?" Marie cried.

Rutherford howled desperately and cowered in the corner, aghast.

Zalman attempted to regain his composure. "I'm fine," he said, groping for his handkerchief. "Other than the fact that my nose is broken, I'm perfectly fine . . ."